Dr Franklin's Island

Ann Halam is the penname of Gwyneth Jones, who also writes science fiction and fantasy for adults. She was born and raised in Manchester, and after graduating from Sussex University spent some years travelling throughout South East Asia. She now lives in Brighton with her husband and son, but spends as much time as she can heading off on adventurous travels.

Dr Franklin's Island

Ann Halam

TED SMART

First published in Great Britain 2001
as a Dolphin paperback
by Orion Children's Books
a division of the Orion Publishing Group Ltd
Orion House
5 Upper St Martin's Lane
London WC2H 9EA

This edition produced for
The Book People Ltd
Hall Wood Avenue
Haydock
St Helens WA11 9UL

A catalogue record for this book is
available from the British Library.

Typeset at The Spartan Press Ltd,
Lymington, Hants

Printed in Great Britain by
The Guernsey Press Co. Ltd,
Guernsey, C.I.

ISBN 1 85881 396 4

1

We formed a small crowd in the big, confused mass of travellers in the Miami airport departure lounge . . . most of us identified by Planet Savers teeshirts, Planet Savers baseball caps, Planet Savers jackets; or at least Planet Savers lapel buttons. We were going to spend the next three weeks together, fifty British Young Conservationists. We were prizewinners in a competition run by the Planet Savers tv programme. Part of the time we'd be staying on a wildlife conservation station deep in the Ecuador rainforest; part of the time we'd be visiting the Galapagos Islands.

I'd enjoyed flying from Gatwick as an unaccompanied minor. It was the first time I'd been alone on a plane, but that hadn't frightened me at all. Now I was beginning to feel scared. I'd won a place on this trip by thinking up a bio-diversity experiment about beetles. But I suppose I'm a typical nerd, good at the details, not very smart at seeing the larger picture. I'd gone in for the competition because I liked my science teacher, and it had been like doing any interesting piece of homework. I had not thought it through. I had never sat myself down and said to myself, 'Hold on, Semirah, what if you win? *You are shy*. How are you going to survive for three weeks surrounded by total strangers?'

Two presenters from the Planet Savers tv programme

were coming with us – Neil Cannon and Georgie McCarthy. They were at the centre of a chattering group, tall, thin Neil with his spiky ginger hair and freckly tan, Georgie with her glowing dark skin and her cheeky smile. Both of them looked very friendly and cheerful and genuine, the way they did on television. They were the only people I wanted to go up and talk to. They seemed like friends, because I'd seen them so often on the tv. But I knew that was an illusion. Real life is different. So I walked about instead, counting my fellow prizewinners.

There were thirty-seven teenagers and ten adult organisers, including Neil and Georgie. There were actually fifty prizewinners, but the other thirteen were travelling on another flight. I decided I was in the rainforest already, or else in a zoo. Maybe I was a new young animal, freshly arrived, and I had to find the enclosure where I belonged. I spotted a baby giraffe, a wolfcub, a slinky green-eyed lizard, a couple of pointy-nosed, mischievous young lemurs; a pouchy-faced boy with tufty auburn hair who looked amazingly like a guinea pig, the kind with the fur sticking up in rosettes. There was one sad girl with big eyes and smooth fair hair sitting by a set of beige pigskin suitcases (while the rest of us had backpacks and nylon stuff-bags), who was like a baby seal – beautifully dressed and totally helpless. There was an awkward, gangly boy with a huge nose, carrying a fluorescent orange puffa jacket, who looked like a new-born wildebeest, stumbling over his own legs. There was a Very Cool Girl, with long black hair, long brown legs, black teeshirt, grey cut-off combats, and a battered rucksack that looked as if she'd borrowed it from Indiana Jones . . . I couldn't think of an animal comparison for her. She didn't look lost or anxious at all. She must be one of the keepers.

But what kind of animal was *I*? I didn't know.

I walked all the way around the zoo, and then came back to a girl with a round face and fluffy hair, who looked like a baby owl. I like owls. I was about to say 'Hello', when along came Very Cool Girl, with her beautiful hair swinging. She smiled at me, and so did the baby owl. But oh no . . . My throat closed up. I simply *could not* speak. I can't talk to strangers! I swerved off, and pretended I'd been heading for a nearby drinks machine.

On the row of seats by the machine there was a big chunky pale boy, with bristle-short dark hair, sitting by himself. You wouldn't have known he was one of us, except that he had a Planet Savers information pack, lying face down on top of his rucksack. I'd given up on the animal identities, so I didn't try to think of one; but I decided I'd sit down, not next to him but a couple of seats away, to drink my can of Coke. I would try to look casually inviting, and maybe we could strike up a conversation. I sat down, giving a sigh that might have been a sort of non-committal half-hello. He looked up, from the game he was playing on his gameboy, and stared at me, narrow-eyed. His expression said very clearly, *I've got your number, unpopular girl. Stay away from me.*

I am not unpopular. People like me when they get to know me. It's just that I'm chubby and shy, and maybe I work too hard, so I'm not very sociable . . . I shrugged and walked away, trying not to feel insulted. But being glared at like that naturally didn't make me feel any better. I decided he was an animal after all; a bad-tempered, solitary kind of animal, liable to lash out and best not approached.

Our flight was delayed. I still hadn't managed to talk to a single person when we got on the little bus and were driven out onto the tarmac to board our charter plane. I'd spent most of my time reading a book (well away from the nasty boy). It was hot outside, even though it was evening by then. I remember looking around at all the grey tarmac and the planes, and the smoggy sky, and being glad I was going somewhere green and wild.

There was some swopping of seat allocations, as the lucky people who'd made friends arranged to get next to each other. I had no part of that. I was extremely surprised when I found I was going to be sitting with Very Cool Girl.

'Do you want the window?' she said. 'I've got it, but I'd rather have the aisle.'

I said yes, I would like the window; and we sat down, me thinking how sophisticated not to want to sit next to the window.

'My name's Miranda Fallow,' she said, holding out her hand. I wasn't used to people shaking hands with me, but from Very Cool Girl it seemed adult and right.

'Howdeedoodah,' I said, 'I'm Semirah Garson, people call me Semi—'

We shook hands. Her grip was thin and hard. My grip was pudgy and shaky, and my palm sticky with sweat. I hoped she wouldn't think I was afraid of flying. I looked out of the window at the fascinating tarmac, miserable with myself for having said *howdeedoodah* like that, and wishing I hadn't told her my nickname, as if she was likely to be interested.

We were flying to Quito, the capital of Ecuador. We were going to stay in a hotel there, before travelling overland to the rainforest base. It'll be all right once we've settled in, I told myself (hoping it was true). We'll be working, helping the scientists, learning about the wildlife. It's easy to talk to people when you're doing something together. Back at home, my brother and my parents were getting ready to go to Jamaica for their summer holiday. My brother thought I was mad to prefer going on a science trip, and I was beginning to agree with him. But I wasn't going to get downhearted. Even if I didn't make any friends, even if I never had a single conversation beyond 'could you pass the graph paper' or whatever, this had to be the trip of a lifetime. Meeting real scientists, seeing the Galapagos . . . The tarmac started to move: slowly as we taxied, then faster and faster until it slipped away from under us, and we were soaring up, with Miami and its skyscrapers, and the huge ocean stretching beyond, all spread out below. Miranda took out a book. I went on staring through the window until we'd reached cruising height.

It had been a long day. Soon my eyes began to close.

I dreamed that I was counting tree frogs. They were brightly coloured, like jewels, but they had too many legs. I was piling them one on top of another. The legs kept sticking out in all directions and I kept trying to tuck them neatly into the heap. It was one of those anxiety-dreams you get when you aren't properly asleep. While I stacked up these frogs that looked like beetles, I still knew I was on the plane. I could hear some people talking loudly. I wished they'd keep quiet, because they were making me lose count . . . The voices kept on getting louder. Finally I opened my eyes.

The window beside me was black. The cabin was dark, except for the fasten seat belts signs, and the little glowing lights that lead to the emergency exits. My eyes felt sticky; I'd gone to sleep with my contact lenses in. I remember peering at my watch, and thinking, *that's funny, I thought we were supposed to be in Quito by now.*

The noisy conversation that I'd heard in my dream wasn't happening in the passenger cabin. The sound of loud voices, shouting voices, using a language I couldn't understand, *was coming from the cockpit.* I looked around at Miranda. She was awake too. We both had our seatbelts fastened; I hadn't unfastened mine since take off. We didn't speak. She leaned down, unlaced her hiking boots, and took them off. Then she reached under her seat and pulled out her bag. I saw her grope in the outside pockets, and transfer some things to the pockets of her combats. I knew, right then, exactly what she was doing, and why . . . I slipped my reefs back onto my bare feet, and bent to fasten the velcro straps. I felt a weird tingling in my stomach and my throat. I badly wanted to go to the toilet, but that didn't seem like an option at the moment. I'd already noticed, with some unsuspected instinct deep inside, that Miranda and I (our seats were in the back, near the tail section) were near an exit; and seen which way we should go to reach it.

'What's happening?' I whispered.

Miranda said, 'I don't know. Sssh—'

They say in an emergency you should drop everything and save your life if you can. But if you can get hold of anything useful, before things go completely bananas, you really should. Take it from me. I couldn't get to my bag. I started trying to reach for my jacket, so at least I'd have my contact lens case, which was in one of the pockets. But it had slipped too far under the seat—

I don't really know what happened next. I'm almost sure I heard a loud bang, like a gun being fired. I know the plane started lurching all over the place, like a car driving too fast on a very bumpy road. Then one of the cabin crew came out of the cockpit as if she'd been pushed out, looking very scared, and there was a strange man behind her, not in uniform, his face covered . . . I *think* his face was covered . . . by a mask. But there was so much confusion. A couple of boys in front of me and Miranda had got up from their seats. I don't know what they were trying to do. A girl started screaming at them to sit down, and the grown-ups had to intervene to break up a fight. It was dark, and I was scared. I concentrated on keeping quiet, not getting involved, hoping I was wrong about what seemed to be happening, hoping whatever was going on would be over soon. Then the plane *nose-dived.* My ears popped so hard it felt as if they were bursting. There was a huge, big roller-coaster scream that went all through the cabin; and I know that would have been the end, *finito* . . . but the plane levelled out again with an ear-ringing shock that was like hitting an invisible brick wall. The undercarriage (no, not the undercarriage, I mean, the belly of the plane, I don't know what it's called), seemed to hit something hard as rock, bounced, and hit again.

'We're ditching in the sea,' said Miranda, softly. 'Let's stick together, huh? Can you swim?' Even now she sounded cool and grown-up, and in control.

There was pandemonium in the cabin, but her quiet voice cut through it. If she'd shrieked like everyone else, I'd never have heard her. I said, 'Yeah, I can swim,' and we got hold of each other's hands.

Things became calmer, now the situation was desperate. The shouting and screaming died off. We were told to unfasten our seatbelts and get out into the aisle. I shuffled for the exit along with everyone else, holding Miranda's hand so tight, you'd have had to cut my arm off to get me loose. Next thing I remember, I was in the water. Miranda was beside me. We were treading water, buoyed up by our lifejackets, in the dark, in a crowd of other bobbing heads and bright blobs of lifejackets. We were trying to get to one of the big yellow life-rafts, but we were being smacked around by waves that were chopping and smashing wildly at us from every direction. Something bashed me hard in the knee. I heard Miranda yell, 'We can't do it! We have to get away from these rocks!' I was absolutely trusting her with my life, so I swam with her, in the opposite direction from everybody around us. And that was very lucky, because it meant at least we were swimming *away* from the plane, when the explosion happened.

I can't remember hearing anything. I was simply flung up high in the air, still surrounded by water, and then deep down, down down . . . and then flying up again, choking and gasping, being thrown about like a rag. Then I was swimming again, with Miranda beside me. My eyes were sore and blinded by salt, my throat was raw, my lungs hurt, and the water seemed cold as ice. I was thinking of the pilot, or whoever it was, who had managed to level out of the nose-dive. I was thinking, I owe that person a life. Whoever managed to do that, doesn't deserve for me to give up now—

Cold black salt water. A blackness overhead lit by brilliant stars. Two heads bobbing near me. Somewhere nearby, a long, steady roaring sound . . . 'Miranda?' I yelled.

'Yes, it's me.'

'Who's that with you?'

Whoever it was didn't answer, maybe they couldn't spare the breath. There was no sign of the liferafts, or any other bobbing heads. The three of us seemed to be completely alone, and I thought of the great huge ocean stretching out forever.

With sharks in it.

'Listen,' croaked Miranda, bumping into me. 'Listen to the breakers. Look, I can see the shore. We can make it. Come on, *swim*.'

Ahead of us I could see a cone of darkness blotting out the starry sky. There was a moving, glimmering line, where that darkness merged with the surface of the sea: I knew this was the foam of waves breaking on a shore. We swam. My wet denim jeans made it feel as if my legs were encased in concrete, and I wished I hadn't put my reefs back on. Miranda had had more sense, taking her boots off. I tried to kick the sandals away, but I couldn't get rid of them. I don't know how I kept on swimming, but I did, for an incredibly long time. When we got in among the breaking waves I was picked up and thrown back, time after time, and that's when I really thought I was done for, because I had no strength left to fight. The water didn't seem like water, it seemed like an enormous, cruelly playful living thing, tossing me about in its claws and its teeth. I was shouting at it, inside me somewhere, *stop it, stop it, knock it off, you big bully* . . . But finally, finally, there was sand underfoot. Finally, finally, on my hands and knees, I crawled out of the waves' reach. Miranda was there with me, and someone else. We rolled over and lay on our backs on the hard wet sand. There was no moon, only the stars, shining blurred and bright; the brightest stars I had ever seen.

'Who are you?' I said, to the person next to me, on the other side from Miranda. I didn't have the strength to sit up and look.

'I'm Arnie.'

'Semi.'

'Miranda.'

All three of us crawled up the sloping beach, until the sand under us was dry. We collapsed again for a while, and then we crawled further, until we came to a big boulder with an overhang; a shelter that seemed, by our present standards, as good as a five-star hotel. There we lay, drenched, battered, too exhausted to talk, too exhausted to sleep, waiting for the light.

2

In the end I must have slept, or passed out. I think we all did. When I woke up it was broad daylight. For a moment the sand was like a soft bed, and I was cosy. Then I moved, and I knew I was terribly uncomfortable. I crawled out from under the rock ledge, wincing when I put my weight on my bashed knee. Miranda Fallow and the boy called Arnie were awake, sitting talking to each other.

Arnie was the big pale chunky boy who had been sitting by himself in the departure lounge.

I went and joined them. I had nowhere else to go.

'Good morning,' I said, awkwardly.

Being shipwrecked doesn't make shyness any easier.

'Hi,' said Miranda, smiling.

Arnie nodded at me, and the three of us sat in silence. I had the impression Arnie and Miranda had been arguing about something.

The beach was a wide curve of glittering white sand, so bright it hurt your eyes to look at it. I couldn't make out any details because I'd lost my contact lenses, but I could see green rugged headlands in the distance, at either end of the curve – like sleeping dragons with their noses buried in the sea. Behind us, all along the bay (which looked to be several miles long) there was a wall of thick, tropical green, that seemed to go straight up into the sky. In front of us, on the blue and shining horizon, there was a line of moving white, with some dark blotches that I guessed must be the rocks of an outer reef.

Great, I thought. My worst nightmare. A beach holiday without even any books to read, with two complete strangers, and at least one of them already doesn't like me.

I pointed at the rocks, 'Is that where we swam from last night? Wow.'

'Yeah,' said Miranda, and she pointed too. 'We did good, didn't we? Look, you can see the plane wreck. The pilot must have tried to ditch in open water, but he came down on the reef instead. Lucky for us we swam in the right direction.'

I couldn't see the plane. But I didn't say so. 'Do you two remember an explosion?' I asked, after a silence that seemed too long. 'When we were in the sea?'

'Yeah,' said Arnie, looking at me sourly. 'The plane blew up.'

'I wonder what happened to all the other people?'

As soon as I'd spoken, I wished I hadn't said that. I decided shy people shouldn't try to make conversation, not even in an emergency. If I manage to talk to strangers at all, nervousness always makes me say the wrong things.

'The liferafts must be beyond the reef,' said Miranda firmly. 'We were thrown onto this side of the rocks by the explosion, but the liferafts were on the other side, I'm sure of it.'

Arnie gave a short laugh.

'We'll have to think of some way to attract their attention,' I said.

The pale boy gave me the same unfriendly stare he'd given me in the departure lounge, only worse, shrugged and looked away. We were castaways together on a desert island, but he was *still* determined not to be nice. I didn't know whether to admire him for being so unaffected by the situation; or dislike him right back. I felt so strange. Yesterday I had been Semirah Garson, a person with a normal life and normal problems. Now I was lost. I might never see my friends, my family, my home again.

I felt a cold shock in the pit of my stomach, *this is real.*

'Okay,' said Miranda. 'Let's start again, now that Semi's with us. Semi, we're trying to work out what happened on the plane, before we ditched.'

'Does it matter?' said Arnie.

'I don't know,' said Miranda. 'But I do know that when you're in an emergency situation, the first thing you should do is put together all the information you have. Anything we remember might help us. Let's each tell the story, see how it fits together.'

So we took turns. I told my story, Miranda told hers. When it was his turn, Arnie said, in a fake little-boy voice: 'I'm Arnie Pullman, this is my story. I live in Surrey. I like computer games and when I grow up I want to be very, very rich. I was on a plane and it crashed. That's it, folks. That's all I know.' Then he grinned sarcastically.

I hated to have to admit it, but he had a point. Miranda, who had been sitting next to me, did not remember what I remembered. It seemed as if we'd been in two different plane crashes. Miranda thought the plane had been lurching around already, when we both woke up. She believed we'd been caught in a tropical storm. She hadn't seen my 'strange man'. She thought the man with the stewardess had been one of the Planet Savers organisers, helping to calm people down. I said there'd been panic, and a fight in the aisle. She said a girl had been taken ill, and the crew had been rushing about dealing with that, as well as with the storm.

13

I was sure we'd been overdue for our landing in Quito, when I woke up. Miranda said she'd looked at her watch too: but she thought we'd been been halfway through the flight time. My watch had been ripped from my wrist somehow when we were in the sea. Miranda was wearing hers. It looked undamaged but it had stopped at 7.35 p.m. . . . But that was *very* confusing, because at 7.35 p.m. Miami-time last night, our delayed flight had hardly left the tarmac. Miranda's watch was not a reliable witness, but that didn't prove I was right. This obviously wasn't Quito, or anywhere in the mountains of Ecuador, but where would halfway from Florida to Ecuador put us on the map? We talked back and forth about time zones, and whether we'd remembered to change our watches, trying to work it out and getting nowhere.

Arnie said he didn't wear a watch. He sat there grinning, listening to us tie ourselves in knots. We were on a beach, in the Pacific Ocean. Other than that, we didn't really know anything. We had no radio, no emergency flares, no first aid, no food or water, and no way of getting in contact with the other survivors . . . If there were any.

Finally Miranda and I gave up. Lots of different dis-comforts started to ooze through the protective cloud of dazed confusion that still filled my head. Miraculously, both my reef sandals had stayed on my feet, but the straps had rubbed my heels completely raw. My clothes weren't dry, they were damp, sticky, and stiff with salt. One leg of my jeans was ripped in half, and through the rip you could see my knee, swollen and bruised, with a big raw scrape. I could feel other bruises too, and my whole body ached from all that swimming. My mouth felt as if it was lined with salted sandpaper, my face felt twice its size, and my hair must look *disgusting*.

'We ought to move out of the sun,' said Miranda at last. 'It's getting hot.'

'We ought to start walking to one of those headlands,' said Arnie.

'And then what?' sighed Miranda. 'It's further than you think, it's *miles*, Arnie, and we have no water. Two of us have no shoes. There's no sign of human life here. If we managed to reach the headland, we don't know if there's a track across it. There might be snakes, there'll certainly be ants, thorns, rocks . . . Have you ever trekked in tropical forest? It's no joke. We'd be lost and bushed in no time.'

'What if there's a tourist village in the next bay?'

'What if there isn't? I say we stay with the vehicle.'

'*What* vehicle?'

'*That* vehicle,' said Miranda firmly, pointing out to sea. 'The plane. Search and Rescue will be searching *for the plane*. If we're not *right here* when they come looking, we are sunk.'

'What if that takes days? Are we going to sit here and starve?'

I guessed this must be the continuation of the argument they'd been having before I joined them. It sounded as if it could go on forever.

'I'm not hungry,' I said, trying to break it up. 'But I'd love a cool shower.'

I'd noticed, while we'd been talking, that Miranda had been looking up and down the beach, calmly *examining* the place. She pushed back her long black hair, which was clinging to her face and shoulders in sticky, salty locks.

'I think that might be arranged,' she said, with a confident smile. She got up. 'Or a bath, anyway. Come on.'

We followed her, Arnie limping and complaining, although the sand wasn't really hot yet. Miranda's bare feet didn't seem to bother her. Before long we reached a stream of water, spreading out into a fan of narrow channels. Arnie looked at Miranda in disgust, as if her having spotted this feature was a deliberate insult to him. He thumped down heavily on his knees, dipped up some water in his hand, tasted it and spat it out. 'Gagh. It's salt.' He smirked triumphantly. 'Nice try, Wonder Girl. But no cigar.'

'We follow it upstream,' explained Miranda, slowly, as if she was talking to a toddler.

When we got to that wall of greenery, the water in the stream was still brackish. Arnie said 'I thought we weren't supposed to leave the vehicle', (you'd have thought he *wanted* to die of thirst). But by then all of us could hear the sound of falling water, cool and clear; and irresistible even to Arnie. We ducked under the branches and picked our way along the bank of the stream, which soon became a clear, dark little river. I had my sandals, with the heel straps undone, so I wasn't too badly off, except that my knee was hurting. Arnie and Miranda managed somehow, with Arnie complaining all the time. It was a relief to be out of the sun, but as tropical jungles go, this wasn't a very attractive example. We didn't see any flowers. A few tall trees with thick rusty-brown trunks loomed up into the sky, but mostly the vegetation was thorny bushes, thorny creepers and giant grassblades that cut our hands when we pushed them aside. We heard birds, and once something (probably a big monkey) went crashing through the branches over our heads. But we didn't actually see any wildlife, except the big ants in the leaf litter, (which we tried to avoid, but Arnie got bitten on his toe once).

After about ten minutes we reached the waterfall. We'd been going uphill since we left the beach. We'd started clambering over rocks: then suddenly, the slope ahead of us became a creeper-hung cliff, with water pouring down it in a thick, silver bright ribbon and churning into a round, clear, pool big enough for swimming.

We stared at it in delight.

'There you are,' said Miranda. 'Your shower, Semi.'

'Watch out for piranhas,' said Arnie. But he almost sounded happy.

I took off my sandals. The three of us clasped hands (this was a foolish risk, and we wouldn't have done it later on); and jumped together into the water.

The pool was nice and deep, and it had nothing nasty lurking in it. None of us managed to touch the bottom. We splashed and we swam, we dived in and out of the thundering spray. We swallowed gallons of pure, fresh water. Then we scrambled out onto the rocks and sat in a row, looking up. The cliff went up like the side of a house. We couldn't see the top of it.

'I don't think we're going any further that way,' remarked Arnie.

Miranda said, 'I'm sure it would be possible. Anything's possible, if you *have to* do it. But we're not going to try, not yet anyway. We're going to—'

'I know, I know, *stay by the vehicle*. Give it a rest. Who put you in charge, anyway?'

'Now I want my breakfast,' I broke in. I hoped Arnie wasn't going to go on like this until we got rescued. Couldn't we try to be nice to each other?

'Ah, breakfast,' said Miranda, grinning. 'For that we go back to the beach.'

About two hours later we were sitting under our rock ledge again, drinking coconut milk, and eating the soft, slippery flesh of young coconuts. Miranda had spotted the grove of coconut palms at the same time as she'd seen the stream in the sand. We'd found plenty of fat, green coconuts lying under them, both the big ones and the little young ones that are really tasty. We'd used her pocket knife (which was one of the things she'd moved into the pockets of her combats, when the plane was in trouble), assisted by various stones and sticks, to break into them. It had not been easy. There had been a lot of trial-and-error bashing, dropping rocks on coconuts from a height, prising and thumping and general frustrated hammering. But we had triumphed.

We had water, we had food, we had shelter from the sun. We had washed ourselves and our clothes free of salt, which might not sound important, but feeling fresh and cool made a huge difference to my ability to cope. For the moment, we had the illusion that we were doing well, and this was a thrilling adventure that would soon be over.

'*Now*, we should start walking,' said Arnie, pointing to the northern headland with a piece of coconut shell. 'That way looks nearer. It can't be more than two or three miles.'

Miranda shook her head stubbornly. 'There are other priorities. We need shelter for tonight. We need to get a signal fire going. We should start work straight away.'

'Knock it off. If I was in a liferaft, I'd take orders from the captain, or whoever. But why do I have to take orders from you?'

'You don't, Arnie. But I'm the one who found us fresh water and food, so maybe you should think about taking my advice. Look,' she added, in a peacemaking tone, 'the tide's gone out a long way. Let's see if we can get to the wreckage. We might find some useful stuff. If we had a water container, that would be a good start.'

Arnie groaned. 'Okay. I'll buy it. Find me my shoes, Wonder Girl. I left them under my seat.'

It was afternoon. The sun was going to disappear quite soon, behind that green wall at the back of our bay. There was a breeze and it was a beautiful, warm, comfortable temperature. As we walked down to the sea together, I had the illusion – again – that everything was going to be all right. None of us mentioned the idea, but I think we were all convinced that we'd get to the reef, and then we'd see the liferafts, and they'd see us. They'd pick us up. We'd be with everybody else. Soon we'd be safe. In a day or two we'd be settling into that rainforest compound with the environmental scientists, and everything would be back to normal.

When something terrifically terrible happens to you, I think your brain *doesn't get it*, for quite a while. You go on trying to see the world the way it was, even when commonsense should tell you that everything has changed forever.

The tide had gone out a very long way, uncovering a strip of flat coral rock that stretched across the lagoon like a causeway. It was painfully rough underfoot, like walking on a giant, petrified panscrubber. I said we could take turns with my sandals, but Miranda said no, I was having enough trouble with my bad knee. She and Arnie managed barefoot. Quite soon we started seeing things from the plane. We came across a rucksack, wedged in among the coral. It was fastened up, but it seemed to have been invaded by some weird, fluffy white sea-creature that was trying to get out.

'What's *that*?' said Arnie, poking it.

Miranda and I took a second look, and started to giggle. 'It's tampons,' I said. 'Expanding widthways when wet—'

'Yecch!' Arnie jumped up and kicked the bag away—

'Don't do that,' said Miranda. 'Pull it out. Anything could be useful.'

So we pulled it out, and threw away the tampons. There was a name on the inside of the top flap, scrolled and decorated in purple ink.

Sophie Merrit. Which was Sophie Merrit, I wondered? Maybe it was my owl girl—

Then it hit me. From the looks on their faces, Arnie and Miranda had felt the same shock. We stared at each other, no one wanting to say what we were thinking.

'Leave it here,' said Miranda. 'We'll pick it up on the way back.'

We went on, in dead silence.

Sophie Merrit's in one of the liferafts, I told myself. They'll all be in the liferafts. But my mind kept showing me pictures of the bobbing heads in the dark water, the jagged rocks, me and Miranda and Arnie swimming the other way from everyone else, that huge explosion. The faces of the teenagers in the departure lounge in Miami started running through my head. I remembered how I'd wandered around, envying the lucky ones in their chattering groups . . . A few metres further on we found a fleet of airline meals, still wrapped in their foil, sealed in plastic bags that had blown up like balloons. We hooked out as many as we could reach and left them stacked on the rock. Then we found a lifejacket, with the straps torn. A Planet Savers baseball cap. Two floating shoes, but not a pair. Neither of them was anything like big enough for Arnie, so we threw them back. Another rucksack (which we salvaged, like the first). A seat cover. A plastic drinking glass. By this time even I could see the silvery shape of the wrecked plane, crumpled on the rocks like a broken toy. It was still a long way off.

The lagoon, which had looked flat as a boating lake from the shore, was heaving with slow, foamless billows, that kept hiding the wreck and the outer reef from view. Arnie started to make a joke about the Swiss Family Robinson, the castaways in a classic desert island story. They manage to rescue a whole department store of supplies from their wreck; we were doing pathetically badly in comparison—

Then he stopped dead – he was in front –; and said quietly, 'Oh, God.'

There was a body bumping against our causeway. No lifejacket. The jacket must have been ripped away by whatever had made the hideous jagged wound that almost cut the torso in two. It was Neil Cannon, the Planet Savers tv presenter. His hair wasn't spiky any more, it drifted like seaweed. His healthy outdoors tan had turned pale and bloodless. He only had one leg.

'I don't think I'll go swimming in this lagoon,' muttered Arnie.

'Can we bury him?' I whispered. 'Can we please, please get him out and bury him?'

It seemed *awful* to leave him there.

'*Look*!' breathed Miranda.

Further out, the billows had lifted into view something I saw as a big, bobbing yellow blur. It was a liferaft! We ran towards it, yelling.

When we were level with it, we saw that the raft was floating upside down. We shouted, in the faint hope that there were people alive, trapped underneath; but got no answer. Then as we watched, it was heaved up by the waves; and lazily turned over. As it rolled, we saw the long wide gash in the bottom, before it slowly sank. 'It wasn't a shark that did that,' whispered Miranda.

'No,' said Arnie. 'It must have been the explosion. Remember, there was an explosion.'

21

'I don't think we're going to reach the wreck,' said Miranda. 'It's too far.'

We stood there, surrounded by the empty sea and the empty sky.

'I think we'd better head back,' I said at last. 'I'm sure the tide's started to turn.'

We returned to the beach in silence, collecting our salvaged goods on the way. I had to close my eyes while we were passing the body. The tide was coming in quickly. We were wading knee deep before we reached the shore, which was very scary.

As night fell, we sat under our rock ledge again, eating more coconut meat and sipping on thin, refreshing young coconut milk. None of us felt like tackling the airline food. In fact, none of us felt hungry. We ate because we knew we ought to. We talked about ways of getting out to the plane. We talked about needing a decent knife, and about making a signal fire. One of the things Miranda had moved from her bag into her pockets, on the plane, had been a box of matches wrapped in plastic; but they were lost. The pocket with them in it had been torn off in the water. We hoped there'd be something we could use to make fire in one of the rucksacks. But we didn't feel like looking now, and anyway, we had no light to see by. There'd been thirty-seven teenagers, ten Planet Savers adults to organise us; and the cabin crew, and the pilot—

Were we the only ones left alive?

'There could still be a tourist village,' said Arnie. 'We don't even know that this is an island. We could be five miles from a road, or something, on the coast of Ecuador.'

Miranda sighed. 'That waterfall was pretty spectacular, wasn't it.'

'So?'

'I didn't see any sign of people having been there. Did you? Not a scrap of litter. No path. There was *nothing*. There's nothing on this beach, either. No footprints, no tyre marks, no fishing nets, no huts. I don't think there's any tourist village, Arnie. I don't think there's a road. I think we're alone, and our only hope is to stay near the wreck.'

'Semi says there was a hijack,' said Arnie. 'I think she's right. There was a hijack, and the plane blew up before the rafts could get away. I don't know how much fuel a charter jet that size carries. I don't know how far off course we could be. But if we're not where we should be, and nobody had a chance to send a radio message before we ditched, chances are that's all she wrote. We're finished if we can't save ourselves. How are your Search and Rescue people going to find us, if they don't know where to start looking?'

It was the same argument as before, but they weren't quarrelling now. They were simply telling each other the bad news.

'Let's go to sleep,' I suggested. 'Things'll look better in the morning, when we're rested.'

We were cold, we tried to sleep. The night passed.

23

3

On the second morning, we thought we heard a plane. We scrambled out from under the overhang and ran about looking at the sky. There wasn't a sign of anything moving, except for a few seabirds over the outer reef, but we were full of hope. We tipped out the rucksacks, and found a magnifying glass; we rushed about collecting dry leaves. Miranda used the magnifying glass as a burning glass, and got a twist of dry tinder alight. I hopped and limped along the shore picking up sticks, Arnie went crashing around under the trees. In an hour or so we had a fire going, and we were throwing green stuff on to make it smoke. Miranda waved a white nylon Planet Savers jacket that had been in Sophie Merrit's rucksack. Arnie ran up and down screaming 'Help! Help!' and waving his arms. The plane (if it had been a plane, and not our imagination) didn't come back. The empty sea and sky looked at us blankly, as if we were mad.

Miranda said, 'Maybe they've seen us, and they can't let us know yet.'

'If there was a plane, you'd think the people in the liferafts would have sent up a flare,' said Arnie.

'Maybe they're saving their flares.' I said. 'For when it's dark.'

We kept the fire going all day, but it was incredibly hard

work. My knee had swollen up and I couldn't walk much. Arnie and Miranda had to do most of the fuel gathering, I did the tending. I felt guilty, but if there'd been three of us bringing in fuel, we couldn't have gathered enough to last through the night. We had to let it go out.

We didn't hear any more plane noises, not even imaginary ones.

On the third day we found the machete. We were patrolling the high-tide line, me limping along with a charred branch for a crutch; looking for more driftwood but not finding any. Miranda and I were collecting scraps of brightly coloured nylon fishing net. Arnie was kicking along a very rusty soft drink can, and saying that these man-made things meant there *must* be people nearby. Miranda told him the sea carries things for thousands of miles. Human rubbish gets *everywhere*, it doesn't mean a thing.

Then Arnie's can hit something that rang like metal. He gave a yell of delight, pounced on something half buried in the sand, and suddenly he was waving what looked like a pirate's cutlass in the air.

'You see!' he shouted, 'You see! Don't tell me this floated over from Australia!'

Miranda, forgetting to be Very Cool for a moment, gave a whoop of joy herself, and grabbed the big knife from him. The blade was hardly speckled with rust. The handgrip, bound in brass wire, was shiny. She turned it over, gloatingly. Then we all saw the remains of an airline sticker, plastered to the metal. You could read the Planet Savers logo, and some of the print . . . saying, 'not cabin baggage'. 'Oh God,' she said. 'The rainforest scientist from Ecuador gave a machete to Georgie, do you remember? On the programme when they announced the competition. I remember, at Miami airport, she told us she was bringing it with her.'

We looked at each other, the shock hitting us again.

Where was Georgie McCarthy now?

Arnie took the machete back and stuck it in his belt. 'I'm going to build a raft,' he said, defiantly. 'With my machete. If you're very good, Wonder Girl, I might let you help me.'

That night we cut our first three notches on the coconut palm tree.

On day four, a snake got into the shelter. Arnie had been hell-bent on starting to build his raft straight away, but Miranda had insisted the first thing we did with his brilliant find was to cut poles and palm fronds, until we had enough material to build a basic A-frame hut. We put it up by the trees. It looked rather ramshackle and pathetic, but we thought it wasn't bad for a first attempt. After the machete find, the hut had taken the whole of the rest of the third day. By the time we'd finished it, stacked our salvaged belongings in there and cut a load of long grass (there was some soft grass, as well as the razor sharp kind) for bedding, it had been dark, and we'd been too tired to do anything but crawl inside and sleep.

In the morning Arnie and Miranda went fuel gathering. When they came back I was sitting in the shelter, out of the sun. Miranda crawled in, and put her hand down on something I'd taken for a curved shadow on the bedding, but it was a snake! She jerked back; it lashed out at her. Miranda screamed, I screamed. We both shot out of the shelter, destroying half a palm-frond wall. The snake came zipping after us. I suppose it was trying to get away, but it didn't seem like it. It looked big, about two metres long, and seemed as if it was out for our blood. Miranda screamed and screamed. I was stunned to see her so out of control. I grabbed the machete from the heap of newly gathered fuel, and I don't know how I managed it, but I was whacking away at the beast. I actually chopped it in half.

The two halves of the snake wriggled in the sand. It wasn't really very big, no more than a metre. It was slim and bright green, which scared me. I knew at least one kind of bright green tropical snake that's deadly poisonous (though I didn't know if you got them in Ecuador). Miranda stared at the wriggling pieces, her face drained and grey.

'I hate snakes,' she whispered. She turned to me. 'My god, Semi! It was *right by you*! Didn't you *see* it?'

I didn't know what to say.

'She can't see anything much,' said Arnie, who was standing there laughing like an idiot. 'She's blind as a dozy bat, haven't you noticed? Semi the semi-sighted!'

'Cut that out, Arnie,' snapped Miranda. 'Don't be such a creep.'

I felt totally humiliated and ashamed. I don't know how many times I'd pretended to see something I couldn't, since the plane crash, and of course they'd known all along. Arnie picked up the front half of the twisting body with a stick. He waved it at Miranda, poking it towards her, obviously hoping she'd scream and run.

'Miranda the scaredy cat!'

'I *hate* snakes,' said Miranda, staring at him coldly, without moving.

He laughed again, and started to chant: 'Semi the semi-sighted! Semi the semi-sighted!' He'd realised he could get at Miranda best by taunting me.

Suddenly, I couldn't stand it. I couldn't stand the whole thing, not for a minute longer. I ran away. I don't know where I thought I was running to. I ran and hobbled and limped along the beach, until my knee gave way, and then I sat there, staring out to sea, crying.

Miranda and Arnie came up after a few minutes, Arnie twirling his snake-stick, Miranda with her shoulders slumped, looking depressed. They sat down near me. 'We shouldn't have built the shelter near the trees,' said Miranda. 'That was my idea and it was asking for trouble. We won't do that again.'

'No,' I croaked, wiping my eyes.

Arnie poked the sand with his stick. 'A grass-coloured snake on grass bedding,' he growled, not looking at me, 'I don't s'pose I'd have spotted it either.'

'I hope there *is* a tourist village in the next bay,' said Miranda. 'Because I've been thinking about it, and I think the initial search operation must have missed us. We might have to wait quite a while now, before they track us down.'

Arnie and I nodded. We'd all been thinking about it.

She leaned back to look at the green wall behind us. 'Plus, I don't think we're going to get up that cliff behind the waterfall very easily. Not without climbing gear. And it seems to stretch all the way along the bay.'

This was as near to being not-positive as Miranda could possibly allow herself to be.

'You mean we're trapped?' I said. 'On a tropical island, without anything to eat except coconuts, between the sharks in the lagoon, and an unclimbable mountain?'

'Yeah,' said Arnie gloomily. 'Prisoners in Paradise.'

For some reason this made us all laugh. It dawned on me that I hadn't thought once about being shy, since the morning after the crash. That made me laugh again, but I wouldn't tell them why. It was a high price to pay, and

Arnie wasn't exactly ideal material, but maybe I had actually managed to make two new friends.

In a really, really bad situation, most people will try not to break down. It's instinct, and if you have any sense, you'll let it guide you. But it's also good, occasionally, to scream and burst into tears and get nasty, for a minute or two. It relieves the pressure. We picked ourselves up, and got to work on moving the shelter. We rebuilt it next to our boulder with the overhang, and it felt more like home there. No more snakes invaded it.

My knee got better, helped by antiseptic cream and a dressing from our first-aid kit (one good thing about having crashed with a planeload of Young Conservationists, those two rucksacks were full of useful survival items). We improved the shelter. We gathered fuel. We made a shadow clock, with a pole stuck in the sand and shorter pieces of wood in a circle round it, like a sundial, and used it to keep track of the tides. We tried various ways of making beach-sandals. None of them worked very well. Miranda lashed her pocket knife in the end of a split stick, using some of the twine we'd collected, and went spear fishing in the shallows. Arnie and I didn't believe this could possibly work. I was so terrified that a shark would come sneaking up and bite her leg off that I couldn't watch. But Miranda came back up the beach with four fat fish, three about the length of my hand, one twice that size. We gutted them and cooked them wrapped in leaves, and they were full of bones, but they were *delicious.*

Apart from the occasional flare-up like the snake incident, the three of us got on quite well. But there was always friction between Arnie and Miranda. The trouble was, he kept having to do what she told him, because although he was annoying Arnie wasn't stupid, and he knew she was right. Maybe even worse, from Arnie's point of view, she practically always kept control of herself and insisted on being positive. It was Miranda who made us keep the signal fire always ready. She was the one who started storing food and making coconut water-carriers, so we'd have supplies to take with us when we set off to explore the island. She had endless plans and schemes for making sure we had plenty to do and think about, and no time to sit around getting depressed. At times I couldn't help sympathising with Arnie. Sometimes it was a relief to have him there, making sarcastic remarks and moaning. But then he'd make one of his nasty cracks about 'semi-sighted Semi', or he'd eat some of our stored rations and lie about it, and I'd hate him.

And the days passed.

The worst thing was the dead bodies. It was bad enough seeing them, but thinking about them was worse. Each of us had our own particular horror. For me it was Neil Cannon, bumping against the coral causeway. Arnie and Miranda helped me try to get him out, to humour me; but it was hopeless. We couldn't get a grip on him, the waves kept carrying him away; and none of us had the courage to get into that water, not even Miranda. So I'd lie at night in our rustling shelter, and every time I closed my eyes I'd see his dead face. I'd see that bloodless, ragged wound, as if someone had nearly sawed him in two, I'd see his hair floating like seaweed.

For Arnie it was the Woman In Stewardess Uniform. There was only the top half of her left when we found her on the beach; and something had eaten out her eyes. Of course we buried her, above the high tide line, but we

30

couldn't make the hole very deep, and Arnie couldn't leave the grave alone. He kept having to go back and check . . . to make sure that nothing had dug her up, I suppose. He didn't talk about it, he just *had to* keep going back there. We'd find him sitting staring at the bump in the sand, looking sick.

For Miranda it was The Girl Who Waved. We thought she was alive when we first noticed her, then we realised that she couldn't be. She was wedged in a reef of rocks that broke the high tide surface, a little way out in the lagoon. I couldn't make out the details, but Miranda and Arnie could, and Miranda had to keep *talking* about it. When the tide was high she seemed to sit up out of the water as if she was sitting up in bed, and the waves tossed her arms above her head, as if she was beckoning to us. But apparently (I couldn't see this, I'm thankful to say) she had no hands. The ends of her arms were reddish fronded stumps, like sea anemones. At night, Miranda often thought she could hear The Girl calling for help. She knew it was her imagination, but she could *hear it*—

And there was the leg, a dreary gruesome sight, a man's leg floating by itself. We didn't think it was Neil Cannon's, it was too fat and white and hairy. It kept reappearing, in deteriorating condition, brought in by the waves every tide, but never ending up on the beach.

We all *hated* that leg.

Every night at dusk we'd go to our notch tree – the most beautiful of the coconut palms, the one that stooped down, in a graceful curve close to the sand – and whoever's turn it was (we took turns, night by night) would cut another notch with the machete. Then we'd sit there telling each other that *tomorrow* the rescue plane would come.

Tomorrow a party of Arnie's tourists would turn up in a glass-bottomed boat, *tomorrow* we'd wake up and see an icecream van driving along the sand, *tomorrow* a helicopter would arrive, full of sexy models in slinky bikinis, for a tropical photoshoot. Tomorrow is another day. It was Miranda who invented the ritual, and started the tomorrow game; and it might sound corny, but it helped.

On Day Five, we woke after a night of wind and rain, to find that most of the wreck of the plane had disappeared from our horizon. There were only a few tattered pieces of dull metal left, hardly visible. That made us feel pretty bad, even me, though I'd never been able to see it. But we tried not to think about what it might mean.

On Day Six, the ants got into our salvaged airline meals, and they had to be thrown away. They were beginning to taste very dodgy, anyway. But this was also an extremely good day, because it was the day we found the wild bananas – which gave us hopes that we were going to find lots of luxurious tropical fruits. This didn't work out, but the thrill of thinking about mangoes and papayas was great while it lasted.

On Day Seven, Arnie made up the 'Prisoners In Paradise' song, with the catchy chorus about *Marvellous Miranda, thinks we can eat sand-a* and *Semi-sighted Semi, walks into a sharkey's belly* . . . and sang it until we seriously wanted to kill him.

On Day Eight, Miranda accidentally speared an octopus, a biggish octopus with a body about the size of a baby's head. It fought back, and made off with our precious, our only pocket knife. We all chased it, splashing, screeching, forgetting about sharks. We caught and killed the octopus, and rescued the knife. Miranda cooked it, but none of us could eat it.

Arnie says octopuses are very intelligent, and now we have committed murder.

On Day Ten, Arnie reckoned he'd finished building his raft. Arnie's raft had been the cause of a lot of arguments. He insisted he only wanted to use it to cross the lagoon and get to the wrecked plane (which we hoped was still there, hidden from us by the rocks), but we knew he secretly planned to set out on the open sea, which sounded like *suicide* in our opinion. For another thing, he kept stealing our supplies. He'd claimed the best of the salvaged fishing twine that we'd patiently knotted into rope. He'd removed the best palm branches from the improved shelter, and cut them up to make his decking. He'd been taking the stored expedition-rations, on the grounds that he needed more food because he was doing the most important work. He took our coconut-shell water containers to use as floats, broke most of them, and lied about it. He half-wrecked my reef sandals, when he borrowed them to go into the thorniest bits of the forest, going after suitable saplings to cut for poles.

Arnie could be fun, but he could be really annoying.

If you said *yes*, Arnie had to say *no*. If you said up, he had to say down. If you were trying to be cheerful, he'd burst your bubble; if you were miserable, he'd laugh. If Miranda wanted to stay by the vehicle, he wanted to trek. If we wanted to prepare for the trek, he wanted to build his raft. Sometimes I enjoyed his sarcastic sense of humour. Sometimes I didn't trust him. All the days I lived on that beach with Arnie, he was definitely my friend, but I never knew if I actually liked him or not.

Anyway, on Day Ten we helped him carry his raft down to the sea and we launched it, on a tether. For a moment, it looked good. We were almost impressed. Then a wave got under it, and it immediately tipped over.

'It's not quite balanced yet,' said Arnie, with dignity. 'It needs some fine-tuning.'

'Arnie,' said Miranda, 'I know you've put a lot of work into it, but frankly I wouldn't care to paddle that thing across a swimming pool. Not with a team of lifeguards on duty. I wouldn't take it anywhere near a lagoon full of sharks.'

'Have you ever *seen* a shark in the lagoon, Wonder Girl?'

Miranda looked at him. 'I've seen the bodies.'

Arnie dragged his raft out of the water and stomped away, pulling it after him.

'What do you want me to do?' he yelled. 'Stay here for the rest of my life? I'd rather die!'

The day after that, Miranda and I went on a foraging expedition, leaving Arnie in charge of the camp and the signal fire. We took with us a coconut shell of fresh water each, some coconut strips to chew, some fire-hardened sharpened sticks, one of the rucksacks, and a netting bag made from the fishing twine that we'd managed to preserve from Arnie.

Miranda was wearing the reef sandals. (The three of us took turns using them, even though Arnie's feet were too big. It was only fair). I was wearing some elegant beach shoes made of coconut husk and string, that didn't really work; but they were better than bare feet. We headed north, along the edge of the trees. We were scouting for the trek to the next bay, which was still our big plan, though even Arnie no longer believed we'd find a tourist village. We were hoping to find another source of fresh water, and also hoping to find more jungle fruit. We hadn't had any further success this way since Miranda's wild banana tree, but we were hopeful.

Our method was to walk along the beach until we came to a natural opening in the trees, then head in toward the foot of the cliff, turn north there and explore until we got stopped by a thorn thicket. Then we'd fight our way out to the beach again and repeat the process. By midday we were further towards the headland than ever before, and we'd found a grove of wild guava trees; but the fruit we'd knocked down with our multipurpose sharpened sticks was too woody to eat. Otherwise, there was nothing to report. It was thirsty work. Even half a day trekking showed us how hopeless it would be to set out on a longer expedition without carrying lots of water.

We rested, chewing our coconut strips, on the cool sand in the shade, and then went on. The forest got nastier; darker and thornier, and soggy underfoot, but never any water fit to drink. After about an hour we hit a gloomy clearing, near the cliff, where Miranda spotted something exciting.

'Look!' she said. 'Something's been digging up the ground!'

We'd seen plenty of birds, butterflies and insects, and one snake. We'd had a few glimpses of monkeys. But all the wildlife on this desert island was very shy. We'd never seen any animals bigger than beetles on the ground. I peered at the marks she'd found, struggling with my poor eyesight.

'And look here! Bark chewed off a tree trunk, and scratches. I wonder what did that? Maybe a small deer? Or maybe it's wild pigs! Ooh, Semi! Imagine roast suckling pig!'

She lifted her head, sharply. I'd heard it too. There was something rustling in the undergrowth, really close to us.

'You stay here,' she whispered, quietly taking out the netting bag. 'I'm going hunting!'

I'd seen Miranda do such amazing things I almost believed she'd reappear in a few minutes with a wild pig slung over her shoulder. I was so hungry for a change from fish and coconut that my mouth was watering at the very thought. I'd been standing there for a few minutes, trying not to breathe aloud, when I heard a snuffling noise behind me. I turned, cautiously, and my heart leapt! In the middle of the clearing there was a pool of stagnant water. There by the pool stood an animal about the size of a large cat. It seemed to be drinking. It had a stripy back, and I was sure I saw a snout. A wild piglet!

I crept forward, holding my breath and levelling my fruit-picking stick like Stone Age Girl The Hunter: feeling incredibly silly, but excited too. The piglet went on snuffling up the dark water. It didn't seem to know I was there. I was almost on top of it when it gave a start, and looked up. I saw its eyes. I saw it lift its front legs, as if to ward off a blow. Oh, *what*? The piglet had *little human hands*!

I screamed.

Miranda came leaping back into the clearing. The piglet squealed. Miranda flung the net bag. The piglet ran through my legs, overturning me, I fell forward, grabbing Miranda. All the birds in the trees around shot up into the air screeching, with a few monkey-hoots for good measure; and we both ended up in the pool, splashed to the eyes in stinking swamp water.

The smell was so bad, we couldn't stand it. We had to give up on the forest, head back out to the beach and wash ourselves down in sea water.

We decided that was the end of the expedition.

I was shaken by the fact that I'd thought the piglet had little hands. But I managed to put it out of my head quite quickly. We were all used to the horrible obsessions we had about the dead bodies, and I think we'd all decided, separately, not to talk about any other strange ideas that came into our heads. It was easier to stay normal, that way.

So I didn't say anything about it to Miranda.

The sky was still blue, but the sun was slipping down behind the mountain by the time we set off for 'home'. The beach was cool. The bay, soft and blurred by my poor vision, guarded by its two sleeping dragons, looked very beautiful, as we walked along beside the water.

'How long do you think it'll be before we really get that roast suckling pig?'

Miranda laughed, 'About a year! That net bag was about as useful as a teacosy!'

'Me and my pathetic fruit-picking stick. I must have looked such an idiot!'

'But maybe we have to learn. We need to expand our food resources somehow.'

We walked in silence for a bit.

'You don't think anyone's ever going to rescue us, do you?'

She looked at me seriously. 'It's getting to be a long time. But we're alive and in good shape, and they'll find us. *We are going to be rescued, Semi.* Don't ever give up hope.'

I knew what she meant. We had to believe. It was the only way to keep sane. I was glad I'd decided not to tell her about the piglet with hands. I didn't want to worry her.

'Tomorrow,' I said. 'The film crew for the next James Bond movie will arrive. This island has been picked out to play the role of the villain's secret hideout.'

'It's good to have something to look forward to.'

'If not tomorrow, then the next day.'

'I certainly hope so. I don't fancy playing Adam and Eve with Arnie.'

We were still snorting and giggling over this idea, as we arrived back in camp.

Arnie was nowhere in sight.

'Typical,' muttered Miranda.

He'd probably gone off into the woods, looking for more trees to chop down. Arnie loved to do nothing. If he wasn't working on his raft, he'd sit daydreaming all day if we let him. Since he'd been *supposed* to sit on the beach keeping watch, naturally he would have decided to do something else. But he ought to be back by now. I wandered about, picking up oddments of our salvaged possessions, that had somehow strayed out of place.

Miranda looked up and down the beach.

'Semi,' she said, worriedly, 'the raft's gone.'

The sun left our beach early. Daylight lasted an hour or two longer; but by this time it was dusk. The moon, which was nearly full, had risen above the outer reef. We went up to the trees, and searched around and called his name. Because it was Arnie, and we were used to his idea of fun, we weren't totally, seriously frightened. We were sure he was hiding, and he'd taken the raft with him to make us really scared. But he didn't come back. When it was getting really dark we started looking for his footprints, or traces of the raft having been dragged off. But it was too late. The moonlight was terribly confusing, and of course there were footprints everywhere. We looked for him at the coconut palms, we even groped our way up to the waterfall pool. But under the trees it was too dark to search; and the beach was empty.

We called his name, over and over, but he didn't answer.

We came back to the camp, shocked and horrified.

We couldn't sleep. We walked up and down by the lagoon, which lay flat and bright and empty under the silver-penny moon. There was no sign of Arnie's raft.

In the morning we discovered that the machete was gone, and our stored food.

'He *wouldn't* have gone out on the raft on his own,' I said. 'He's not that stupid.'

'Then where is it?' whispered Miranda.

Out in the middle of the bay, The Girl Who Waved flapped her ragged arms, as if she was signalling to us that she knew where Arnie was.

She knew.

4

On Day Thirteen, at low tide, I went out along the coral causeway alone, wearing the reef sandals, watching carefully where I put my feet. There are some very nasty creatures that live in the holes in coral rock. It was something we did regularly, this trip, to see if more stuff had drifted in. Strange oddments kept on turning up: shoes, bits of clothing.

Neil Cannon's body had gone. I reached the place where it had been, and stood looking down. The water was deep beside the causeway there. You could see through the sunlit layer that was like liquid air, into depth on depth of clear blue darkness. I shivered in the hot sunlight. Since the night of the crash the sea had seemed like an enemy to me, a monster lying in wait, going to kill me if ever I gave it a chance.

A few metres ahead there was a dark blob, bumping against the rock. I felt sick. I thought it was a human head.

Oh God, I prayed. Oh please, don't let it be . . . Don't let me have to see that.

It wasn't Arnie's head. It was a Planet Savers jungle-kit water canteen, the strap waving vaguely to and fro, the cap fastened tight. I knelt down. The foamless billows lifted the canteen, and gently carried it out of reach. I knew the sea was trying to lure me, trying to make me lean out too far and fall in. But I wasn't going to be caught like that. I waited, patiently; and the canteen came bobbing back. As I reached to grab it, a great, long, torpedo shape came gliding upwards, out of the blue. The shark turned over. It was very close. I saw its pale underbelly. The U-shaped, serrated, gummy gape of its mouth opened, lazily, and shut again: and then I was hugging the canteen in my arms, so terrified I didn't know how I had managed to get hold of it.

I knelt there feeling sick for a minute or two. Then I walked on. I knew if I lost my nerve for this reef-walk once, I'd never get it back. The point which we'd established as the furthest we could go, without getting trapped by the tide, was marked with a long pole. As I reached it, I found a clean blue plastic barrel, floating half-full of sea water.

Miranda was sitting outside the shelter, splitting up some palm leaf. The three of us had been weaving ourselves sleeping mats. Miranda had taught us how.

'Hi,' she said quietly. 'Any sign of the raft?'

I shook my head. I put the canteen and the barrel down in front of her.

'I saw a shark,' I said. 'Big one.'

My mouth began to tremble. I sat down beside her, and both of us started to cry. We sat there hugging each other, and crying, until it was time to go and cut the sunset notch.

Three days later we gave up searching and waiting for him, and set out on the trek to the next bay. We took our sleeping mats, the extra clothes, all the food we had and all the water we could carry. In case the Search and Rescue people arrived while we were away we left a message, written in pebbles on the sand above high tide, and a big arrow of sticks and stones, showing which way we had gone.

It took us a day to get to the headland and (I think) four days to climb it. We did a kind of imaginary version of the notch ceremony every night. We'd say we were going up to the notch tree, say who was cutting the notch, and play the *tomorrow* game. But we might have got muddled. We weren't writing anything down. There'd been a pencil case in one of the rucksacks, a ballpoint and the remains of a notebook in the other; and a couple of sodden paperbacks. But none of the pens would write, so we'd used all the paper for tinder once it dried out. The signal fire had seemed more important.

Of course there were no tracks. We reckoned the headland was about a hundred metres, or three hundred feet high – which doesn't sound like much, but it was very hard going. We ran into thickets we couldn't get through, cliffs we couldn't scale and gullies we couldn't cross, and worst of all we lost the compass almost straightaway when I fell into a ravine. Every time we had to back-track we'd end up getting lost and going round in circles, because we couldn't see the sun for the trees. When we reached what seemed to be the top, there was no viewpoint. We had to struggle on, through ant-ridden thorny thickets, for another day, and sleep sitting up under a tree because there wasn't a piece of ground clear enough for us to lie down. The next morning we managed to get a clear view into the northern bay. It was as empty as our own, but there was no beach. Swampy forest went right into the sea. We discussed trying to find a way down, but there didn't seem to be much point, and really we had no choice but to turn back. We'd run out of food and water.

The night we arrived back in camp (which we counted as

the night of Day Twenty), there was a storm. Our shelter was wrecked, and we lost some of our most important possessions. At least The Girl Who Waved was gone in the morning.

Miranda told me the last bits of wrecked plane fuselage had gone too.

Later on we tried the southern trek. The southern headland was further off, bigger, incredibly rugged and totally covered in thickets with thorns like razor wire. We didn't make it to the top. We both lost our footgear. By the time we got back to camp we both had deep, bleeding blisters, and Miranda had a huge thorn buried in the ball of her left foot. My sore knee, which had never got completely better, had swollen up again and started to ooze yellow stuff. We got the thorn out, but the wound on Miranda's foot had festered until it looked nearly as bad as my knee, and our blisters wouldn't heal. We'd lost all the first-aid in the storm, so the only medicine we had was rest.

For days after that, we did nothing but what we absolutely had to do to stay alive.

Our morale had never been so low. We'd never felt so utterly wretched and defeated. But it was in that time, after the expeditions, that I first *really* made friends with Miranda Fallow. While Arnie had been with us, he'd been like a weight in the middle of a balance bar. He'd kept us together, but in a way he'd also kept us apart. We'd been friends and allies, but Miranda had still been Very Cool Girl to me, someone so distant and admirable she was not quite human. When we were climbing the north headland and the south, we'd been as down as two people could be, and come through only by clinging to each other. There

43

was no distance left between us, by the time we got back. There was no fear.

Maybe you have to be naturally shy, to know what I mean by that.

We spent most of the time talking, when we were sick: we had nothing else to do. Miranda told me about her parents, who were both anthropologists. How she'd travelled with them in all sorts of wild places when she was a child, but now she was at boarding-school, which was okay . . . but lonely. I told her about my great-grand-mother's farm in Jamaica, which is the place I most love on earth; and my aunts, really my great-aunts, who never got married and don't like children underfoot – which means that when we go there on holiday my brother and I run absolutely wild.

I told her about being shy. She told me about having parents who are so high-powered and so interested in each other that you can't possibly compete.

We talked about ambition (we both wanted to be scientists), friends and enemies, tv and music. We talked about sex and romance, and life, and death.

We never talked about being stranded here permanently. We had to keep hoping.

Little bad things happened (the ants got into my patent ant-free food storage). Little good things happened (we found more wild banana trees; I speared my first fish). Neither of us got our period, which was a blessing. I think it was because we weren't eating enough. I wasn't chubby any more, and Miranda was like a sun-burned skeleton.

We kept on cutting the notches as best we could, with Miranda's pocket knife. In a way I wished we could stop. I didn't want to think about how much time had passed, how little hope there was left of rescue. But it would have been hard to give up the ritual.

Sometimes I'd look at her and I'd think: you?

You?

It's very weird to meet someone, another girl, on a plane, and it turns out she might be your life's only companion.

Forever.

On Day Forty, we were feeling better. Our feet had healed up, and we'd had good luck with our fishing, so we'd eaten well the night before. We'd been taking it in turns to hobble up there and get water, but we hadn't had a swim in the waterfall pool since before the expeditions. We decided that today we were strong enough. So we set out, wearing coconut husk clogs tied to our feet with rags; and taking with us our water canteen, and some fish-coconut-wild-banana lunch. Me in my cut-off denims and the white Planet Savers jacket that had belonged to Sophie Merrit, Miranda in her tough old combat shorts and her black teeshirt. These were our best clothes. Since Arnie had gone, we hadn't worn anything much at all, on the beach. I think we'd dressed up to celebrate feeling stronger again. We weren't exactly expecting to meet anyone.

We reached the pool, stripped off, had a swim and got dressed again. For something to do, Miranda started looking for ways to begin the climb that we'd long ago decided was impossible. I wandered around poking at the leaf litter, thinking I might try digging for edible roots. Miranda pulled herself up, under the falling water, into the cleft in the rock that was as high as we'd ever been able to reach.

'Hey, Semi,' she called, in a very strange, questioning, sort of voice. 'Come here?'

I went over, and she helped me haul myself up. She pointed.

'Do you see what I see? Or am I imagining it?'

We could both see a strand of bright orange fishing twine, caught on a projection in the rock wall, deep inside the cleft. I looked at her, and nodded. 'I can see it.'

'My God. You see what that means? Arnie was here! Arnie was *in there*!'

'I don't believe it,' I whispered.

Miranda groped in the pocket of her shorts, brought out a small shell, and tossed it into the dark. It vanished, with a rattling sound. 'I'm going to try and get further in.'

'Be careful,' I begged. '*Please* be careful.'

She squeezed herself upwards and inwards. 'It gets wider . . . oh, I'm *through*!'

I followed her. We were in a narrow, wet, black passage. The first few metres must have been a tight fit for Arnie, but then it got a little wider. The air was fresh. We could hardly see a thing. We groped along, me very scared that we'd get stuck, and then, when I was going to suggest turning back, there was light ahead.

A little more groping, and we were in a tall, narrow cave, looking out of it into a hidden valley. We'd decided long ago that our island (if it was an island) must be volcanic, and the cliff at the back of our bay was probably the side of an extinct volcano cone. This valley must be inside the crater. That was astonishing enough, but *there were buildings below us.* Modern, concrete buildings, not grass huts.

'Wow!' breathed Miranda. 'Civilisation!'

She kept on staring, mesmerised, telling me the details that I couldn't make out. Roads, fields, a big fence, a helicopter pad, something that looked like a *football stadium,* with floodlights! I looked around the entrance of the cave, hoping for more signs of Arnie. Something glinted, peeping out from a mass of creepers. I jumped, because I was afraid it was a snake. But it wasn't. It was . . . I got hold of it, hardly able to believe my eyes. *It was the machete.*

'Miranda!' I gasped.

I stood there, holding Arnie's machete. My heart was beating like a drum. Arnie had come through here, *nearly thirty days ago,* dropped his machete, gone down to those buildings. But why hadn't he come back for us? What had happened to him?

'Hey! Miranda!'

She'd gone. For a moment I thought she'd vanished, like Arnie. Then I heard her calling, 'Semi! Come down here, I've found a road!' I followed her, through the lush undergrowth, clutching Arnie's machete, and soon we were both standing on a graded, stony jeep track, with our mouths open and eyes popping in amazement.

'We're saved! We're saved!' yelled Miranda. We grabbed each other, jumping up and down and shrieking. Then we heard the rumbling of an engine. A big jeep was coming up the track. It stopped. About a dozen men in pale-coloured uniform jumped out.

I stared at them, stunned. Miranda yelled, 'Hurrah!' or something.

The men were big and brown-skinned, they had round curly heads. Their faces were blurred blanks to me. They talked to each other in a language I didn't understand, and I began to feel that something might be wrong. They didn't sound friendly. It flashed into my mind that maybe they were soldiers. Maybe we'd stumbled on something secret, like a military radar station. But surely they couldn't blame us.

We couldn't help being castaways.

'Semirah! Run!' yelled Miranda.

The men had grabbed her. They shouted at me, and pointed at the machete. 'Oh, this?' I said. 'Oh, it doesn't mean anything, it's not mine.' I threw it aside. Two of the men jumped at me, and I started to struggle. One of them hit me on my arm. It felt like a punch, but it must have been an injection of some kind. Suddenly I was looking up at the sky. My bad knee hurt where it was twisted under me, and then everything went black.

5

I woke up in a bed. It felt very strange, after sleeping on palm fronds on the sand for so long. I wasn't comfortable. I felt lost and uneasy, as if I wasn't attached to the earth any more. I lay looking at the tight white sheets, trying to remember how I'd got here. I was still dressed – and that puzzled me, because I seemed to be in some kind of hospital. I turned over and saw that Miranda was beside me in another bed. The room we were in was long and bright, with white painted walls. Tropical sunlight streamed in through the windows. Though we were lying next to each other, she was out of reach. There were bars between us, floor to ceiling.

There were two rows of five beds, exactly like a hospital ward. The other beds were empty. Each one of them was caged in bars. Miranda turned over, and looked at me.

'What's going on?' I whispered.

'I don't know. I didn't last much longer than you did. I tried being quiet and obedient, but they knocked me out anyway . . . You should have run for it when you had the chance, Semi.'

'Oh, sure,' I said. 'Either they'd have caught me, or I spend the rest of my short lonely life back on the beach, eating sand and playing with the sharks. No thanks.'

We laughed, and sat up. We were both still wearing our ragged 'best clothes', we were still dirty and sweaty and salt-crusted. No one had brought us any food or water. There was nothing in our cages beside the beds, no bedside cabinets, not even a light switch.

'How did we get here? Did you see anything on the way?'

'No,' said Miranda. 'I was knocked out by the cave, the same as you. Those men grabbed me, they grabbed you, they put us in the jeep and and I woke up here just now. I don't remember anything else.' She got out of bed and looked at the bars. The door to her cage was locked, not with a padlock but with a swipe card box that had a keypad of buttons. 'Well, we're still prisoners, but I don't think we're in paradise any more.'

'That's an improvement, anyway,' I said, bravely as I could. 'I was sick of paradise.'

I got out of bed too. My door was locked, the same way. We stood looking at each other, two dirty sunburned skeletons: with the bars between us.

'Maybe it *is* a prison,' said Miranda. 'An Ecuadorian High Security prison, on a lonely island with no other inhabitants. That would make sense. This could be the prison hospital. I suppose they put us in here because they didn't know what else to do with us.'

'But they'll let us go? Surely they'll let us go?'

'Of course they will. Don't be daft. Can you speak Spanish?'

'No. I can speak a bit of French; and I can speak Jamaican, I mean, you know, Jamaican-English, if that would help. That's all.'

'I only speak French and a bit of German. I think they're speaking Spanish.'

'But *someone* will understand English. Won't they?' I pleaded.

'Bound to. People speak English everywhere. We'll be on our way home soon.'

We were both frightened. There was something *weird* about all this. But Miranda was much better at keeping it down than I was. We heard footsteps approaching the door of the ward. We jumped back into bed, and lay there. It seemed the wise thing to do.

The man who came into the room looked like a doctor. He was wearing a white coat and carrying a clipboard of notes. He was white. He had wire-rimmed glasses, yellowish hair that was going thin on top, and the kind of skin that never turns colour in the sun, it just keeps on going red and peeling.

'Good,' he said, standing outside our cages, 'you're awake.'

It should have been a big relief to hear him speak English. But it wasn't. Maybe it was the way he looked at us – though I couldn't see his expression clearly. Maybe it was the tone of his voice. He didn't sound as if he was talking to two half-starved, ragged teenage girls, who had turned up somewhere they shouldn't be. He sounded . . . extremely different from that. He sounded cold, angry and also (which was very weird) *afraid*. When you can't see people's expressions too well, you pay a lot of attention to their voices.

'Where are we?' said Miranda. 'What is this place? Is this a prison?'

He gave a short laugh. 'No. The island is private property. You were caught trespassing.'

'But we couldn't help it! We were shipwrecked, I mean plane-wrecked. Look, we're sorry we were trespassing, but

51

we've been stranded for over a month. We have to get in touch—'

'No need to worry about that at the moment. Come along.'

'We're very hungry,' said Miranda, 'and thirsty. And please can we use a bathroom?'

He unlocked our cages, 'This way,' he said, shepherding us ahead of him out of the door, 'we want to give you a medical check.'

There were two of the big brown-skinned men in uniform, in the corridor. We went along with them willingly, we didn't want to be knocked out again. Miranda kept on asking questions, but neither the men in uniform nor the doctor took any notice. We were taken to a room like a doctor's surgery, the men in uniform stayed outside.

We were allowed to use a bathroom then. We went in together. Neither of us felt like staying outside alone with the strange doctor. It was an ordinary small bathroom, with a toilet and basin and a shower and a mirror. I felt like a visitor from the stone age, sitting up on the gleaming white porcelain throne, and I was so nervous I couldn't make myself pee. We stared at ourselves in the mirror over the basin, trying different angles and holding up our legs and feet to get a view of them.

'What a sight,' muttered Miranda. 'Look at our toenails! Look at our *hair*.'

'We look like very thin Flintstones.'

'We look like mad fakirs in India.'

If there'd been a window, I think we might have tried to wriggle through it. But that would have been stupid. 'We'd better go out,' I said, 'before they come in after us.'

'We're on our way home,' said Miranda, firmly. 'Soon.

52

For certain.' We squeezed hands, and returned to face our mysterious, scary rescuers.

Another of the big men had come into the surgery, this one dressed in a white coat like the doctor. He seemed to be a nurse. My feelings kept going up and down, bouncing like a yoyo. When the doctor said 'medical check', I thought everything was going to be all right. That sounded like a normal thing to do with two castaways. But when the medical check was happening, it *didn't feel right*. We were weighed, and our eyes looked at and our throats looked at, our reflexes checked. Our body fat (such as it was!) was measured with callipers. The doctor-man looked at my knee; at our feet. The nurse-man took blood samples, at which point I had to sit down very quickly. I suppose I was so pared-down I didn't have a millilitre of blood to spare.

Then came the really strange part. We had to do a sort of IQ test, on a printed sheet.

'What's this?' said Miranda. 'What on earth's going on?'

'Please do as you're told.'

'Look, we're not applying for jobs here. We were ship-wrecked, our plane crashed. We want to go home.'

'You'll understand why we need this information, later. Please fill in the questionnaire.'

So we filled in the questions, which were general knowledge and things like do you sleep well, do you make friends easily, do you think you react well in emergencies.

'Maybe it's to see if being plane-wrecked made us go crazy,' whispered Miranda.

We had to swallow hysterical giggles.

The doctor and his assistant were wearing plastic gloves, so they didn't actually touch us. They never looked us in the eye except when they had to; and hardly spoke to us. There'd have been more contact between a vet and a couple of sick rabbits. *And they were afraid.* I knew that, with every instinct. This gave me an extremely creepy feeling.

'You're both in remarkably good shape,' said the doctor at last. 'Considering that you've been living on the beach, entirely on your own resources, for well over a month, you're in very good shape indeed. A recalcitrant infection in that left knee, but it's not going to be a problem.'

'You knew we were there?' said Miranda.

We stared at him, completely astonished.

'Oh, yes,' said the doctor, shrugging, 'of course we did.'

So then we knew. It was like waking up in the dark on the flight to Quito, and seeing the fasten-seat-belts signs, and hearing shouting in the cockpit. *This is it.*

We're in trouble.

But what kind of trouble could we possibly be in?

Miranda went on staring at him. 'What's your name?' she asked.

'Skinner,' he said, biting his lip. 'You can call me Dr Skinner. Wait here.'

He went away. The big nurse, who was wearing one of those pale uniforms under his white coat, stood watching us, with folded arms. We didn't like to speak to each other. I had the same weird tingling in my throat and stomach, that I remembered from the night of the plane crash.

After a short while, Dr Skinner came back. 'Dr Franklin will see you now.'

'Who's Dr Franklin?' asked Miranda.

'The owner of the island. My boss. Come along.'

'Someone owns this whole island?'

'As I told you. This is private property.'

'He must be very rich. Is he famous? Is he English like you?'

He laughed again, short and contemptuous. 'So many questions,' was his only answer. Our guards (they seemed like guards) followed us to the end of the corridor, where some automatic doors opened, and we were outdoors, in a big courtyard. The first thing I noticed was that it smelled like a zoo. Then I realised it *was* a zoo. There were long rows of cages, and several houses for bigger animals, with a sleeping block in the back and a fenced run out at the front. In the distance I could see a paddock with blurred brown shapes in it. Horses or maybe deer. The courtyard was well-cared for, the pavement was clean, there were trees and flowering plants, but the smell of captive animals was very strong. I saw a couple of the pale-uniform men moving around; they seemed to be tending the greenery. They took no notice of us.

All these cages made me think of the bars in the prison ward.

Dr Skinner didn't hurry us. He let us look. The first place we passed was a small corral where a few animals like little fat deer, with blunt muzzles and coarse gingery fur, were standing around doing nothing. 'Capybara,' said Dr Skinner. 'Native of Argentina, related to the guinea pig. Very stupid.' One of the Cabybara was sitting alone, next to the fence, in a strangely human posture. As we approached it got to its feet and turned to look at us. It had the same blunt muzzle as the others, but its lips were puffy and red, which looked very odd. It made a miserable slobbery sound, and shuffled off towards the sleeping house, moving slowly and awkwardly. Miranda caught her breath. Its back legs, though they were covered in ginger fur, looked as if they'd been put on the wrong way round. They were dumpy, dwarfish *human* legs – with human feet.

We stared at Dr Skinner. He smiled unpleasantly, and moved on.

The next enclosure smelled of pigs. There was a huge dark-coloured bristly sow in there, lying on her side. She looked normal. Her stripy piglets, who were scrabbling around fighting to get at her milk-teats, were like the piglet I had seen in the wood. They had human hands. The way they squealed and chattered at each other, in high-pitched almost childish voices, made me feel sick.

'Take your time,' said Dr Skinner. 'Why not? Take a good look at all our curiosities. You may learn something.'

There was a dark, covered passageway, night-lit, where a colony of things like bats stared at us from behind glass. They had leathery wings and pointed, animal faces, but they were hanging the wrong way up, (for bats). Their naked, pale little human legs dangled down, kicking aimlessly at the air.

There was an aquarium, where something that looked like a monkey-head with octopus tentacles crawled around and around its tank, looking very bored and completely terrified, if that combination is possible. In another tank a group of lobsters (I couldn't see what had been done to them) sat gazing at us, like the live lobsters you sometimes see in a seafood restaurant.

There was an aviary of bright-coloured parrots, some of them normal, some of them with floppy miniature human hands or feet or patches of human skin, sticking out between their breast feathers. The poor birds were tearing at these growths with their beaks. The floppy hands and feet reminded me of the shark-chewed limbs of The Girl Who Waved. Next to the aviary, in a run with some bare branches propped together as a sort of climbing frame, there was a spotted jungle cat, all alone. It wasn't weird to look at, not in any way that we could see, but it crouched in a corner of its cage, its front paws over its cat-face, moaning softly.

'Is this what you do?' said Miranda, finally. 'You collect freaks? But what for?'

'We don't collect them,' said Dr Skinner, with a tight-lipped smile. 'We create them.'

'You *create* them? How?'

'Gene grafting. Surely you've heard of genetic engineering?'

'But what are you trying to do?' I demanded. 'What's the point in it? Are you trying to turn animals into humans? That's just cruel.'

'Animals into humans? No!' Dr Skinner laughed with contempt again, as if he couldn't believe my stupidity. But in his voice I heard fear, horror and fear . . . 'The animal experiments are steps on the way to a much greater goal. They were all essential to the project. We don't cause needless suffering. But we've gone beyond them now. Have you seen enough?'

We nodded, very uneasily. He took us indoors again, through another door, out of the heat and into air-conditioned coolness. It was a relief to get away from the zoo-smell. But I was beginning to think I must be asleep and having a bad dream.

Dr Skinner tapped on a door, and a voice called, 'Come in!'

The room was like another doctor's surgery, only grander. A man, another white man, got up from behind a big desk and came out to greet us. He looked about fifty or sixtyish. He was tall, he had broad shoulders and rather long, thick, grey wavy hair, almost to his shoulders. It framed a broad tanned face with a big nose and a wide, thin mouth. His eyes were very bright. I noticed them, when he came close to shake my hand.

Later on, it was always his eyes that I remembered.

Later on, just thinking about those bright, cold eyes would make me shake with terror.

'Ah, Miranda, Semi. I'm very pleased to meet you at last.'

He shook our hands. He had a rich, smooth, calm voice, and an American accent.

'Do sit down. We have a lot to talk about.'

'First things first,' said Miranda, briskly. 'Apparently you and Dr Skinner know that we've been stranded on your island for ages. So you must realise we need to get in touch with our families. We need to contact the authorities, the British Embassy, tell them we're okay and get ourselves taken back to Quito, or wherever is nearest. Is Quito the nearest city? We don't know where we are. We don't want to put you to any trouble, but we need your help. We want to go home.'

Doctor Franklin chuckled, and smiled broadly as if she'd made rather a good joke. He sat down again behind his desk. 'I don't think we'll be contacting "the authorities" just yet. Do sit down.'

So we sat down.

When I first saw Dr Franklin, I was relieved. I didn't like his eyes, but he seemed like a normal person, not spooky and mad like Skinner and the guards. I thought, thank goodness, at last we've reached someone in charge, now we'll be okay. But the moment I saw that smile, the relief began to drain out of me. I didn't have a clue what was going on, but I knew there was something very, very wrong with this man. With everything.

'In good health,' he said, leaning forward, steepling his hands and beaming at us over his fingertips. 'Highly resourceful, psychologically very resilient. Good! Excellent!'

'Resilient?' I repeated. It wasn't that I didn't understand the word, it was because I couldn't understand why these compliments sounded so creepy.

'It means you bounce back, young ladies. You don't crawl into a corner whimpering, when you're faced with a tremendous challenge. You deal with it. Now, Dr Skinner tells me you've been asking a lot of questions. Naturally, you want to know what we are doing here. Let me see. I'd better start by finding out what you know.'

'We don't—' I began. I was going to tell him we weren't interested in what was going on, and we didn't want to know about his nasty experiments, we wanted to leave. At once. But Miranda kicked me and shook her head a little, so I stayed quiet. I remembered what she'd said to me and Arnie on the beach, long ago. Any information might be useful.

There was a glowing white screen on the wall behind his desk. He tapped some keys on a keyboard in front of him, and an image appeared there.

I couldn't make it out much.

'Can either of you tell me what this is?'

'I think it's a photograph of some human chromosomes,' said Miranda.

'Ah! Good, very good. Excellent! And do you know what chromosomes are? Semi?'

'What DNA comes in,' I said. 'The sort of packets that DNA comes in, in the nucleus of a cell.'

'Good. Now then, do either of you know what *transgenic* means?'

'It's genetic engineering,' I said. 'If you insert different genes, or parts of genes, into the chromosomes in a cell, and you can get the cell to accept them and make them work, then the plant or animal or whatever will develop differently. It will be a transgenic organism. Like, you can make crops that are resistant to weedkiller, so you can spray the whole field and only the weeds will die. We've done a bit about that, in school.'

'Good, very good,' said Dr Franklin again, with his creepy beaming smile. 'But as you have seen, on the little tour Dr Skinner gave you, *our* work is of a different order. We are tackling a much greater challenge, much more exciting than tinkering around with vegetables. We are . . .' He stopped, and smirked, 'Well, not to let false modesty get in the way, let's say *I*. I, with the assistance of Dr Skinner, am on the brink of producing transgenic human beings. Think about it! See if you can picture some of the possibilities. Imagine being as strong as an elephant. Imagine being able to use sunshine to make food, like a plant. Imagine being able to fly like a bird. Imagine being able to breathe underwater, and swim with the fishes. Imagine . . . though this is further off, I admit, being able to breathe different gases, or live comfortably in the hard vacuum of space.'

He paused and stared at us expectantly. I nodded, and I saw Miranda doing the same. I wondered if she was feeling as bewildered as I was. I had that tingling feeling in my throat and stomach, stronger than ever. I looked behind me. I hadn't realised it before, but Dr Skinner was still there, at another, smaller desk, making notes on a laptop computer.

It was like being on a mad, horrible school trip. We'd had the tour, now we were getting the talk from the person in charge. Dr Franklin started to tell us about his first human trials, which he said were about to begin. He was planning to build a human-bird and a human-fish. He said there were very good technical reasons why certain kinds of animals were among the first he would attempt, but happily they were also forms with most exciting advantages, for the future of the race—

Miranda and I managed to exchange a glance, while he was pointing at his screen. We didn't need to speak. The message *he's mad,* passed between us loud and clear. We both turned to look at Dr Skinner. He knew we were looking at him. I saw his forehead and his ears turning redder than ever. But he kept his head down, and kept on tapping away at the keys. It was obvious we would get no help there.

'So, which would you like best to be, Semi? Miranda? A bird, or a fish? In my case, I think *flight* would be the great attraction. If I had your young cells, but alas it's too late. Would you like to make your choice now? Or shall I tell you more?' said Dr Franklin.

We wanted to get out of here. But that wasn't on the menu.

'Please, tell us more,' said Miranda faintly.

So Dr Franklin told us more. He told us that the idea of growing a new kind of human being from scratch was a non-starter, and everyone who was trying that kind of research was a benighted fool. Chances of success were much greater with his special secret method, that nobody else had tried, of putting new genes into a ready-made living human body, and getting it to change. He'd proved this with his animal experiments. He told us how he could inject artificial chromosomes into the bone marrow, and then the normal cells in the body would be rapidly replaced by cells with different DNA, that would take over and change the whole organism. Like cuckoos in the nest! he said (and laughed loudly, at his own joke). He told us how a human skeleton would become a fish skeleton, with the bones turning to cartilage; or, in the case of the bird transgenic, the bird-person's bones would become hollow and 'gracile' (that means fragile and slight). How the bird-person's blood would be altered so it could process more oxygen, because flight takes a huge amount of energy. Oxygen is the fuel the body burns to power its muscles, and a bird has much bigger muscles, relative to body-weight, than a human. How the fish-person's limbs would fall off or fuse together, and gills would grow in the person's neck. How the lungs would be changed, and the livers, and the skin . . . Images, blurred and meaningless to me, kept flashing up on the wall screen. Sometimes he'd swing around on his chair, and point at them with a laser light pen.

I kept thinking that we ought to ask questions. Maybe we could get on the right side of this mad man, by pretending to be keen about his insane ideas. But Miranda had gone very quiet, and I couldn't make myself speak. My throat had closed up, and my ears were ringing. I felt as if someone had given me a huge smack around the head. Dizzy, dazed, sort of otherworldly, as if I was going to faint. It had to be a joke. Surely, this must be a joke. He couldn't really be planning to do the kind of unbelievable things he was describing to real people. Either it was a joke, or I was dreaming. I felt like crying, or bursting into hysterical laughter. Every so often he'd stop and wait, staring at us with those bright eyes; and we'd nod at him madly. That was all he seemed to expect.

At last he stopped, and didn't start up again. The screen went grey. It was over.

'Any questions?'

Miranda said, stubbornly, 'When can we call our parents?'

Dr Franklin looked pleased. He chuckled, and shook his head.

'Full marks for persistence, Miranda, and for keeping your own interests in mind. Well done. You may go now. My assistant will give you each an information pack. Study the literature carefully. Dr Skinner, you can take them back to the ward.' He came out from behind the desk and shook our hands again.

'I'm very pleased to have such excellent candidates for my first human trials. Fortune smiles on me. Well, fortune always favours the brave, they say. Now you should get some rest. You have a big day tomorrow. And remember, you're totally free to make that choice.'

Dr Skinner walked us back through the zoo again. He stopped by the capybara enclosure, and stared at the one with human legs and human lips.

'Where d'you get the human genes from?' said Miranda, her voice expressionless.

He looked at her with a sneer. 'Where do you think? From humans. Originally some of the DNA was mine, and some of it was his. Rebuilt, of course . . . lately we've been using DNA cultured from tissue samples taken from our employees' children. Young cells are essential for the kind of work we're doing now. The kids don't know what we're doing, they don't suffer any harm. A scraping from the inside of your cheek, or a small blood sample, never hurt anyone.'

Miranda nodded. 'But why the lips?' she whispered (as if she didn't want the poor capybara to hear). 'Why the back legs? It seems so pointless. What's the advantage?'

'It doesn't work like that, Miranda. Transgenics can be rather . . . random. Sometimes we don't know until we see the results, what part of the animal is going to change.'

'What happens if you change something so it doesn't w-work any more?' I quavered.

'We've had plenty of losses. And some survive, in very twisted forms. But our goal is to take humanity beyond all the limits. Of course there's a price to pay.'

He walked us on.

'Where do you get the animals?' said Miranda. 'Are they wildlife from the island?'

'Some,' he said. 'The pigs, the parrots, the bats, the snakes. Others we buy.'

'You mean you have a supplier, who makes deliveries? By air, or by sea?'

Dr Skinner smiled that thin smile again. 'You never give up, do you Miranda.'

'Do all the people in uniform live on the island?'

'Oh yes,' he said. 'With their families, and all the amenities. Dr Franklin treats his employees well. They're very loyal to him. They wouldn't help anyone who wanted to leave without his permission. That's definitely not worth considering.' And he laughed.

When we got back to the ward the guards stayed outside. Dr Skinner handed each of us one of the plastic folders that he'd been carrying since we left Dr Franklin, showed us into our cages and locked the doors. Then he stood looking at us with horror and pity. Exactly the way we'd looked at the weird animals in Dr Franklin's zoo.

We stared back at him.

'This is crazy,' said Miranda at last. 'You can't keep us here, Dr Skinner. What your boss is doing to those animals is horrible, but it's none of our business. We're not going to tell anyone. You have to let us go.'

'We've got family, we've got friends,' I babbled. 'You can't keep us prisoners—'

'Oh yes we can, Semi. Think about it. Try to put two and two together. Your charter plane crashed forty-five days ago, off course and some time after sending an emergency message that appeared to indicate a massive mid-air explosion. We've been in contact with the Search and Rescue operation. They found no survivors, no wreckage, and when their search widened to include this area, we were able to tell them nothing. No one's looking for you any more. We've been waiting until we were sure of that, but if you hadn't found your way to us, we'd have been coming to pick you up soon.'

Have you ever been afraid you were lost? When you were little – at a fairground, or in a crowded shopping centre maybe? Maybe you remember how at first you didn't realise what was wrong. You were sure the next person you ran up to would be your mother, the next big man-shape you saw would be Daddy. But the strange faces look down at you, not Daddy, not Mummy; and you run away from them. You start running faster, as if by running you can catch up with the normal world that was all around you a few minutes ago; and be safe. In the end you're running through the crowd of big people, tears pouring down your face, frightened to death.

'We didn't know how we were going to tackle the human trials,' he said, watching our faces. 'But you are ideal. You are missing believed dead. You don't exist.'

But things are even worse than you imagined, not just lost, lost *forever*, but . . .

Cold tremors went through me. The monstrous truth was dawning on me, and I knew why Dr Skinner had looked so afraid, so horrified, right from the first moment—

'He's not really going to experiment on *us*!' I gasped, in utter disbelief. 'Not *really*!'

'I'm afraid he is.'

'What if we say no?' said Miranda at last. 'Will he kill us?'

'*Kill* you? Certainly not. What use would that be? Doctor Franklin is going to *change* you, the way the animals you've seen were changed. You are the next stage. You won't "say no". You won't be asked for your consent. Didn't you hear me? You don't exist.'

'You can't let this happen,' said Miranda. 'We're innocent human beings.'

He laughed, bitterly, 'Is there such a thing as an innocent human being? I don't think so.' He ran his hands through his thinning hair, and wiped the sweat that had gathered on his forehead, although it was cool in here. 'I've tried to put it off,' he muttered, staring at us as if he hated us, 'but it was bound to come to this. We've gone as far as we can, infusing human genetic material into dumb animals. Don't you see? We can't exactly advertise for teenage volunteers for this, can we? But *we have to have human trials.* It's the only next step.'

'Then experiment on yourselves!' snapped Miranda.

'I said, *teenage.* Haven't you been listening to a word you've been told? We are too old, Dr Franklin and I. This is the way it has to be, and you can forget about appealing to my better nature. I have none.' He came closer to the bars, his voice rising hysterically. 'He's a genius. He's crazy, but he is a genius. You'll serve the cause of human progress. You will become more than human! Look on it as a great adventure.'

'I don't believe this,' said Miranda, flatly. 'It's not going to happen. You are not going to let it happen. You'll keep us for a few days, you'll talk Dr Franklin out of his crazy idea, and you'll see that he lets us go. Now can we have something to eat?'

He shook his head. 'No. Nothing to eat. An orderly will bring you some water. You'll be having your pre-med early tomorrow morning. The initial bone marrow extraction will be done under general anaesthetic.' He started to walk away, then he turned back. 'Oh, by the way. Don't try pleading with our orderlies. They don't understand much English, and if they did, they accept completely Dr Franklin's right to deal with trespassers. I told you, Miranda, they are very loyal, all of them. They know our work here is very secret, very sensitive. I think they have, ah, an idea that we are connected with the US government. It isn't true, but it's a useful story. They will not help you.'

One of the men in uniform came, with a carafe of water and two paper cups. He waited while we drank, and took the cups and the carafe away. He didn't speak to us. We didn't speak until he was gone. I looked at the bars of my cage. How thick they were. I wondered why Dr Franklin had made them so thick. Why did the beds have to be in cages at all? What did he think would happen, when he started turning human beings into something 'more than human'?

At last Miranda said softly, looking at the floor of her cage, 'When Dr Skinner came to fetch us, he knew we were awake. Let's see if we can spot the cameras.'

We paced up and down, saying things that didn't matter. I said, 'He thinks we were forty-five days on the beach. I wonder when our count went wrong—'

'Maybe it didn't, maybe we're right, and he's trying to confuse us—'

'I wonder if it's still Day Forty. Maybe it's Day Forty-One. I'm hungry enough. We don't know how long we were knocked out for.'

'I think it's still Day Forty.' She glanced at me, and

nodded slightly. She'd found the camera lens, peering down on us from a slot high up in the wall. We took the two information packs and sat on the floor, up against the bars that separated us, with our backs as if accidentally turned to that spying eye; and kept our voices low. There wasn't much point in this. The true horror was that our captors *didn't care* what we plotted against their schemes. No more than if we'd been two guinea pigs planning a break-out. But it made us feel a little bit better.

I turned the pages, occasionally muttering something to Miranda. But I couldn't take in anything. I dropped my spinning head in my hands.

'Oh, Miranda, this can't be real,' I whispered. 'Can it be? Is this real?'

'I hope not,' she said grimly. 'I hope it's a nightmare and we'll wake up safe on the beach, alone with those nice friendly sharks in the lagoon. But if it's a nightmare it's very realistic, because *he's* real. Doctor George Franklin. I've heard of him.'

'What do you mean, you've heard of him?'

'From my parents. You remember, I told you about them. They're anthropologists.'

'That means they study people, doesn't it? What's that got to do with genetic engineering?'

'Nothing much. But a few years ago Doctor George Franklin was famous, in science. He had all kinds of ideas about how humans might be changed, in the future, by genetic engineering. The same sort of thing as he was saying to us. Imagine if people could fly, imagine if people could live under the ocean. People listened to him, even though the things he was suggesting were completely impossible back then. And they still are, as far as I know . . . But he's very rich, he inherited a huge fortune, so he didn't need

68

anyone's approval. He ran his own projects and paid his own scientists to work on his weird ideas. I think he was even a futurology consultant or something to the US government, for a while. Then he got prosecuted for doing some cruel experiments on chimpanzees. That was the end of his public career. My parents and their friends used to use his name as an example of a mad scientist, science gone bad. That's why I remembered.'

'Is that why you went all quiet, back in his office?'

'Yes.'

'He's crazy, isn't he?'

She nodded. 'Yeah. I think you could safely say that.'

'And Skinner's mad too. The way he looks at us . . . the things he says.'

'Yes. They're definitely both insanc.'

'But they can't *experiment* on us. They just can't, *they just can't.*'

'I think we have to work on Dr Skinner,' said Miranda. 'I think what happened over the chimpanzees was that one of Dr Franklin's assistants had an attack of guilty conscience, and blew the whistle on him. We have to get Skinner to do that.'

'I don't think so, Miranda. I think he used to have a conscience, but he strangled it.'

'He cares about the animals,' said Miranda. 'I know he hates us, because we make him feel so guilty. But I was watching his face when we were walking around the zoo. He's sorry for them. And he's *afraid*.'

'Yes, I noticed that. Well, of course he's afraid! His boss is going to . . . going to make him murder two teenagers, basically.' I swallowed hard. I still couldn't possibly believe those two teenagers were us.

'Mm. I wonder what Dr Franklin has got on him, to keep

him here. Maybe he's been in trouble with the law, maybe he's been thrown out of respectable science too, and this is the only job he could get. But he must be lonely. He must be starved of friendship. We'll have to try and get him to talk, make personal contact.'

It's what you're supposed to do, if you get kidnapped, or if you get trapped by an evil psychopath. You're supposed to talk to the attacker, humour them, befriend them, make them realise that you're human so that they can't do what they planned. That's the kind of strange thing, like how to be a castaway, that you learn from films, from newspapers, documentaries, from the tv news . . . But never in a million years do you think it would happen to you. A faint hope rose in me. Maybe, maybe it could be done. Miranda had saved me so often. Maybe she could even save us now—

I thought about those animals. The capybara with the human lips, the parrots plucking at the growths on their breasts, the bats with tiny, dangling human legs. Suddenly I remembered something.

'*Miranda*, I saw one! I saw one of those piglets with hands!'

'What do you mean? We both saw them—'

'No! Ages ago, before Arnie disappeared. That day we went foraging—'

I told her what I'd seen in the northern woods, by the pool in that dark clearing.

'Why didn't you tell me about it?'

'Because I thought I was seeing things. And then Arnie—' My eyes filled with tears. Miranda was being tough and calm as ever, but I was losing my grip. 'The truth is I didn't want you to know,' I wailed. 'I didn't want you to know I was having hallucinations. I was always the weak link, wasn't I? You and Arnie, you were both okay. He was big and strong, and you . . . you can do anything. But I was useless, I knew I was. Remember the snake in the shelter? I nearly got you killed that time—'

I was breaking down, beginning to sob. I couldn't help myself.

'Oh, come on. The snake probably wasn't even poisonous. I'm stupid about snakes, that's all.' She slipped her arm through the bars, took my hand and squeezed it. 'You were not useless! Who invented the shadow clock?'

'I didn't think of that myself. I remembered it out of a book.'

'You remembered lots of brilliant things. What about the ant-proof food storage?'

'The ants got into it.'

'Yeah, but only at the very end. And you invented the firebox.'

'I didn't. I just thought of making one. You made it. If I'd told you about that piglet, we'd have known something weird was going on. We'd have had warning.'

Miranda shook her head. 'Nah. I'd never have believed you. How could anyone believe something like that? What could we have done, anyway? We were trapped. They'd have come to fetch us in the end, if we hadn't found the passage.'

Silence fell. It seemed as if we'd run out of things to say.

'Hey,' said Miranda at last. 'If your piglet escaped, maybe we can escape too—'

'We'll have to hurry,' I said. 'We're going to be operated on in the morning.'

The room had grown dim. Outside, the brilliant sunlight was fading into the swift tropical dusk. Soon it would be night. I wished I knew if it was Day Forty or Day Forty-One. This seemed to matter a lot. If this was my last day on earth, I would have liked to be able to think I'd still been free when it began. A free castaway, a prisoner in paradise. But I had no way of knowing.

Operated on in the morning.

She kept holding on to my hand, and I kept on holding hers, but each of us was alone, a million miles apart. I saw my 'information pack' lying on the floor. I let go of Miranda's hand, grabbed it, and threw it away from me so it whammed against the bars. As if I cared what kind of a monster I was doomed to become. Yes, that was it. Better face up to the truth. There was no escape. Either we were going to be tortured to death, or we were going to be turned into monsters. Depending on whether Dr Franklin was a crazy genius, or plain crazy. I got up and flung myself on the bed. Miranda lay down too.

We didn't cry, we didn't talk any more. We just lay there.

6

Someone was shining a bright light into my eyes. My brain dissolved into a puddle of terror. I thought this was it, Dr Franklin had come to take me. Then Dr Skinner turned the penlight beam the other way, shining it on his own face. 'Come on,' he snapped, in an angry undertone. 'Get up, let's go.'

When he'd hustled me out of bed, he grabbed my pillow and shoved it down under the sheet. It was dark in the ward, but I could see that Miranda was out of bed too. When she saw what he was doing she did the same thing with her pillow. He let me out and then her, and shut the cage doors behind us. The three of us slipped out into the corridor, and he locked the door of the ward too. We walked along to a recessed panel in the wall, which he opened. He pressed a couple of buttons. I thought, 'He's turning the security system back on . . .' and it was only then that my brain caught up, and my heart leapt.

He was helping us to escape! We were going to escape!

'Come on,' he hissed. 'Don't mess around. Keep up.'

Miranda and I were barefoot, Dr Skinner seemed to be used to walking silently. We followed him swiftly along dark corridors, then through some automatic double doors into a big dark hall. There were long tables, chairs. Light gleamed faintly on glass-fronted counters. It seemed to be a canteen, or a cafeteria. He pointed to us to sit down at one of the tables, hissed, 'not a word from either of you,' and went off. We stared at each other, two shadowy faces, the dark making my eyesight as good as Miranda's. Our hearts were beating hard in hope and fear.

Dr Skinner came back, with his arms full. 'Not a word,' he repeated. 'Listen.' He still sounded as if he hated us. 'I'm going to let you out of the compound, you're going to make your way to the east shore. There's a motor launch. There'll be no one in it, it will be moored against a jetty. You get into that launch and hide yourselves below, in the cabin. You will be taken to the coast, the mainland. Then you'll be on your own. You'll have to walk. Head north. You'll find a place called Menozes, where you can find someone who will understand English. Say you were ship-wrecked on an empty atoll, there are a few around here. Say you built a raft, say you floated for days. Say you lost everything and you have no idea where you were stranded. Say what you like, but *I'm saving you*, so don't you tell any secrets about what happened to you here, don't say any-thing about what he planned to do. Is that agreed?'

We nodded, frantically, and tried to whisper our thanks.

'Don't thank me. I don't even think you'll get away. The people at Menozes will send for Dr Franklin when two castaways turn up, he's a big man around here, the local *jefe*, you know what that means? They'll send for him, and you'll be back.' He set his teeth and grimaced, as if he was in pain. 'He wants to study the psychological effects. Do you understand me? I'm warning you, he doesn't only want to change you, he wants to play games with you as well. *Do you understand me?* I don't know why but I think . . . in a way . . . that's what I really can't endure.'

We stared at him blankly. We didn't have a clue about

these 'games'. We were worried about being killed or changed into monsters.

'Here, take these. Food and water. Come on.'

He shoved a backpack at each of us. We struggled to put them on as we followed him, walking fast and silently again through the dark hall, through a room with gleams of metal and smells of food that must be the kitchen, and out into the night.

We crossed a pitch-dark, overshadowed yard that smelled of rubbish bins and petrol, and came to a door in a wall, where Dr Skinner stopped and tapped buttons on another keypad. Through that door, and we were in Dr Franklin's zoo. I could smell the caged animals, I could hear rustlings and faint chittering sounds. As we passed the aviary, a parrot gave a sleepy squawk, and then the jungle cat started crying. Beside me, Dr Skinner started and drew his breath sharply.

'It does that,' he muttered, 'It does that all the time. We don't know why. We gave the pair of cats an infusion that did something to their brains. We don't know what we did, and it can't tell us. Its mate died, it howls. Sometimes it goes on all night and all day. I wish I could kill it, but he'd find out, and he never wants them killed. Never, he always wants to keep his pets alive. It's unbearable. It would drive a sane man mad. Can't hurt me though. I hate the racket, that's all.'

He wasn't talking to us. He was talking to himself.

We crossed the zoo, and left by another door. Then we were outside all the buildings. I could see the stars overhead, each of them given a glowing halo by my miserable eyesight. I was glad to see them again. Dr Skinner pressed on. Every few seconds he'd switch on his penlight, and flash the white beam around us.

Nothing stirred.

'Quickly,' he muttered. 'I have to get you through the perimeter fence, and then I have to get back to the buildings and switch the fence back on. He makes his rounds at night. My boss doesn't need sleep. At midnight he takes a break from work, comes out and walks around the compound, checking every building, every door, it's a habit with him.'

His pace had speeded up, we were half running to keep close to him. I could feel dry stony earth and stalks of rough grass under my hard, bare feet.

'There's a gate in the fence, and a footpath leading through the mountain side. It's a short cut to the launch mooring, the kitchen staff use it. When you get to the boat, *hide*. Don't try to speak to the man who'll be taking it to the mainland, don't show yourselves. Our technicians know more than the orderlies, about what goes on, but don't push it. He'll help you but he doesn't want any trouble with the boss.'

I was thinking about movies I'd seen of people escaping from prisoner of war camps. I was praying the floodlights wouldn't come on, praying there'd be no sirens, no voices yelling at us to stop. Now we'd reached the fence. There was a small gate set in it. There was an ordinary padlock, no buttons to tap. We waited as he fumbled with the key. He was still muttering under his breath, almost sobbing.

It howls I heard, and then, *oh god, howls, and it's only an animal—*

Miranda and I looked at each other, 'I think he's drunk,' whispered Miranda. 'I smelled his breath. Whisky. Dr Skinner,' she said aloud, 'you'd better come with us. Think about it. He's bound to know that you helped us escape. You have to take this chance.'

I knew she wasn't thinking of Skinner's well-being. He

had to come with us. If he stayed behind, hysterical and jabbering like this, he'd be telling Dr Franklin all about our escape, ten minutes after we'd gone. Now he'd dropped the key. He got down and crawled on his hands and knees, scrabbling for it in the grass.

'You'd howl,' he was mumbling. 'I know you would. You'd howl too, you girls, and I have no conscience, but I can't stand that noise—'

He stood up again, with the key. The penlight beam reflected in his glasses, giving him two mad white pennies for eyes.

'But there'll be others,' said Miranda quickly. 'He'll get hold of some other teenagers, and they'll howl too. You said, it's bound to happen. Come with us. You've been brave so far, you planned everything really well. Now be braver still. Leave him.'

'I can't leave. You don't know him. He'll know I let you go, but he'll forgive me. He needs me. It's not easy to find a scientist of my calibre who is . . . who is . . .'

'So hard up for a job that he would torture children,' Miranda finished for him.

Dr Skinner flinched, but he was beyond being insulted. 'This is my great work,' he whimpered, swaying on his feet. 'You don't understand. This is *the work*. It must go on! Except that you'll howl, you see. I can't stand the idea of lying awake at night, listening—' At last he'd managed to unlock the padlock. He held the gate open. 'Go on, go. Go!'

We couldn't risk arguing with him any longer. Miranda had grabbed my hand, we were in the act of darting through the gate, leaving Dr Franklin's hateful compound—

When the floodlights came on.

It wasn't actual floodlights, it was the headlamps of two big jeeps. They were parked about a hundred metres away from us. They'd been invisible in the darkness. Dr Franklin was standing beside the nearer of the two, with a party of the uniformed orderlies. Some of them were holding big flashlights. Some of them had guns in their hands. Dr Franklin shone his light over our faces, and then fixed the beam on Dr Skinner.

'Well, Charles,' he said, in that calm, smooth cheerful voice, 'I had a feeling you were going to try something like this. Inevitable, I suppose. Luckily forewarned is fore-armed—'

The light had paralysed us, but the sound of that voice spurred us into desperate action. We ran together through the open gate, into the mouth of a narrow footpath between high banks. Fronds of greenery leapt out of the dark and smacked our faces as the men came pounding after us. We pelted down the hillside, barefoot on sharp stones, looking wildly for some way to leave the path . . . straight into the arms of more of Dr Franklin's men.

He was like that, Dr Franklin. He liked playing games. Maybe he'd wanted to catch Dr Skinner in the act of helping us, to give him a scare. Maybe he'd forced Skinner to pretend to be helping us, so he could test our 'resilience'; or soften us up so we'd give them no trouble in the morning. It didn't matter much, either way. We'd never had a chance. He'd known exactly what Dr Skinner would do. He'd known exactly what was going on. We were brought back. Miranda kept pleading with the big men, begging them in English and French to have pity, to think of their own children, to let us go.

It had no effect at all.

Back into the brilliant mesh of white beams, the jeep headlamps and the flashlights. One of the orderlies locked the gate behind us. Dr Franklin took out a mobile phone, pressed buttons on the keypad, listened for a moment and said something in Spanish. Then he said to us in English, in a kindly tone, 'The power is restored to the fence, young ladies. Remember this, if you try to escape again. It would be irresponsible of me not to protect my experiments, so that fence is electrified. Do not ignore this warning!'

I felt as if I was standing on a stage, one of my worst nightmares. Two big men held my arms. The other uniformed men were staring at me without pity from behind the lights. Dr Skinner was huddled up beside Dr Franklin. He'd taken off his glasses and he was wiping them, carefully, over and over. Dr Franklin was smiling. He wasn't angry with us for trying to escape. We couldn't make him angry. We were experimental animals.

I thought I could hear the jungle cat howling, though we were far away from the zoo. I could see those blurred images on the screen in Dr Franklin's office, I could see the drawings and computer images in the information folder. Those were pictures of *my body*. Those hideous changes would be happening to *me*. I knew I was helpless in the grip of someone who was truly evil. I had to scream or my chest would have burst open. I think Miranda was trying to calm me, but it was as if she wasn't there. I started to fight. I know I bit a man's arm until I tasted warm salty blood in my mouth, I know I got free.

Dr Franklin had said *the power is restored*.

The words flashed on me like a promise, the only possible promise of escape. I ran and leapt for the towering wire mesh, praying the voltage would be enough to kill me.

But the fence didn't fry me. Dr Franklin had been lying. I climbed until I lost my grip. As I fell, I heard Dr Franklin saying coolly, 'Well, *now* we can switch the power back on. That was very interesting! I see we'll have to be careful how we deal with you, Semirah.' The orderlies carried me back to the prison-ward, with me screaming and punching and biting and kicking at them all the way.

They knocked me out again. When I came back to consciousness I was in the prison ward, in bed. I'd been washed. I felt clean, and I knew I wasn't wearing my tattered old castaway clothes. I had bruises all over, same as the morning after the plane crash. I could feel that one of my eyes was closed by a throbbing lump. I tried to sit up. I couldn't. I tried to free my arms from the tight sheets. I couldn't. I finally opened my eyes as best I could and looked down at myself. In the grey light of another dawn, I saw my body wrapped in a whitish linen jacket, with the arms crossed in front and fastened at the back. The material was tough and stiff. It was a straitjacket. Across my chest there was a thick rubbery band, pinning me to the bed. There was another band at my waist, another across my legs, and two loops fastening down my ankles.

I don't know how to describe the horror of that waking.

'Miranda?' I whispered.

'I'm here, Semi.'

I turned my head, and saw her through the bars, strapped down the same as me.

'Oh God, Miranda I'm *sorry*.'

'What for?'

'They wouldn't have tied you down. This is my fault.'

'It doesn't matter. Semi, listen. This is going to happen. We can't stop it.'

'Oh, God please—'

'No, don't cry, listen. The only thing to do, is we *must accept our fate*.'

I couldn't stand this. I was going to start screaming and

screaming and this time I wouldn't stop until I was out of my mind. I would die insane, howling like that jungle cat as they tortured me. But Miranda kept talking. Her voice was a light I could follow, like the little glowing lights that led to the emergency exit.

'Listen, Semi. This experiment is exciting. *Exciting*, do you hear? Say it.'

'Exciting,' I whispered. I didn't understand, but I was trusting her with my life.

'We're going to be made more than human, we're going to have superpowers.'

'I want to go home.'

'Well, you can't go home. That's over, that's out. So concentrate on the adventure. Skinner's right, you know. Sometimes, to move science forward, people have to take tremendous risks. Imagine going up in the first aeroplane. Imagine being in a space capsule, with nothing outside but a hard vacuum. Something goes wrong, and you have to deal with it, however terrified you are, because nobody back home can help. So, we're going to imagine we've volunteered for this. The straitjackets are to . . . to keep our muscles rested, before the operation. We've volunteered, and now we have to be brave, really really brave and tough. That sounds good, doesn't it. Doesn't it sound good? I like the idea of being brave.'

'We're going to die.'

'Yes,' she said, with a shake in her voice. 'Probably. But we don't have to die screaming. Let's go for quality of life? For believing anything that makes us feel better? Come on, Semi. Try it.'

'Quality of life,' I repeated. 'Volunteers.' I remembered that plunge into the cold sea, and Miranda beside me yelling, 'Swim the other way!'

'So, which do you want to be?' she whispered. 'Fish or bird? We're supposed to choose. Do you want the freedom of the ocean? Or the sky?'

I'd been afraid of the sea, since that horrible night. But I could remember too much about the things that would happen, to change someone into a bird. Skeleton changes, growing new muscles, new blood. All I could remember about the fish was gills in the neck. That didn't sound too bad. 'I want to be the fish,' I said, feeling an awful coward. 'I'd rather be the fish, if I have to be one or the other.'

'Good,' said Miranda cheerfully. 'Because I've always wanted to be able to fly.'

I said, making a huge effort, 'What kind of bird would you like to be?'

'I think I fancy being a hyacinth macaw. They're the rarest parrots in the world, I'll be worth a lot of money. And I'll be a beautiful colour. Turquoise blue, my favourite.'

'Macaws are clever as well. Supposed to be as clever as a three year old child—'

'Yeah,' said Miranda, 'that sounds like me.'

and we giggled—

I don't know how, but she had us giggling—

'I want to be a shark,' I said firmly. 'A great big, Great White Shark, and I'll bite Skinner's bum. I'll bite his bum *off*. Hey, maybe you should be a golden eagle, or what about a condor? Something fierce and big.'

'Maybe I'll be a nightingale. Next to flying, I've always wanted to be able to sing. I can't sing a note as a human being.'

'I think being a fish will be like flying too. I'll be flying in the ocean skies. Maybe I'll be able to talk to dolphins . . . How long d'you think we've got before they come for us?'

'Not long. Let's keep talking. Which ocean would you like to be a fish in? Arctic, Atlantic, Pacific? I read somewhere that Antarctic fish have antifreeze for blood, so you won't feel the cold. You'll be able to swim under icebergs, it'll be so beautiful—'

'No thanks. I'll take the Caribbean. I'll seek for pirate treasure.'

'You can adorn yourself with it, you can be a Great White Shark with diamond earrings—'

We knew we weren't going to get turned into a *real* fish and bird. We knew we wouldn't end up looking like natural animals, even if the experiment didn't kill us. But it was better to talk about sharks and nightingales. Imagining ourselves as strange monstrosities, human sized mutant-things, was not going to help.

Terrible things happen every day. You read about them in the newspapers, you see them reported, you watch the movies. Serial killers murder people, children get tortured. Not all of it is fiction. The bad things have to happen to someone, in real life, sometimes. As bad luck would have it, it was my turn, and Miranda's turn. And why not? Why should we be protected? We lay there talking quietly, and gradually I started to accept.

The bogeyman had got us. We'd fallen out of the space capsule of normal life, into the cold, cold dark that surrounds it, where only death is waiting. Nothing could save us: but we didn't have to die screaming.

I found out that as long as I didn't move at all, I could keep the panic under control. I could pretend I was lying still because I wanted to lie still. I breathed a few times, practising. Then I thought of myself inside my body. I imagined a little person, no bigger than a match, walking up inside my chest, (as if I lived in my heart) up through my neck and into my head. There was space in there. My arms were free, there were no rubbery bands pressing me down. My little person had plenty of room, she could sit in an armchair and watch tv—

'I'm pretending I'm lying still because I want to lie still,' I said.

'That's a good idea,' said Miranda. 'I'll try it.'

'I'm pretending I've walked out of my body and gone to live in my head for the moment. I'm going to sit inside my head, relaxed, watching imaginary tv.'

'Brilliant. Thanks, Semi. Tell me if you find a good programme.'

Time passed. The morning light got brighter. At last we heard footsteps, and Dr Skinner came into the room. We watched him coming up to our cages. He looked sick and horrified, I was pleased to see. He needed a shave, too. We lay quiet and watched him. When he came up close, Miranda said softly.

'I'd rather be me. I may be going to die by torture, but I'd rather be me than you.'

He behaved as if he hadn't heard her speak. One at a time, first me and then Miranda, he injected us with something, in our necks (which was the only part of us he could easily reach). When the needle went in to me, and I knew there was no hope left at all, I nearly, nearly lost it. I whimpered, on the edge of screaming—

Miranda whispered, urgently, 'Semi, hey, there's something I forgot. Arnie's here.'

Dr Skinner was wheeling a stretcher trolley in from the corridor—

'Yes,' I whispered back. 'I think he did get here—'

'You found the machete in the cave . . . and Dr Franklin knew our names. It went out of my head, because there was so much else going on, but of course this is what happened to him, he was caught the same way we were. That's why he vanished. He has to be around, somewhere.'

'No, Miranda. Arnie's dead. I've thought about it too. That's why he never came back. They've experimented on him and he's dead—'

'No he *isn't*. Believe it! He's alive and he's going to rescue us.'

I knew she was talking nonsense, deliberately, to help me. But it still helped.

'He'd better hurry, he's got about three seconds to come bursting in.'

No time for more.

I was going first. I couldn't bear to say goodbye in front of Dr Skinner, so I tried to smile everything I felt. I was beginning to feel woozy. Skinner rolled me onto the trolley. The ceiling started to go by.

I thought about the pilot who pulled out of that nosedive. I thought about everyone who had died in the plane crash. I thought about other teenagers in the world, and children, lots of them younger than me, who'd had to lie on a trolley with the ceiling going by, on their way to have terrible things done to them. Children in real hospitals where the doctors were good and kind, but sometimes that made no difference. Sometimes terrible things happened anyway. The children had to be brave. I could be brave too.

But most of all I thought about Miranda.

Then I was in another room, with green walls and bright lights. I was on stage again. A plastic mask was put over my face. I heard Dr Franklin's calm, smooth voice telling me to count backwards from ten. A great adventure, I thought. Exciting. Here I go.

7

Day Forty-Two.

I was not dead. Nothing hurt. I was in a room with no bars. There were two beds, and two bedside cabinets with an electric lamp standing on each of them. The walls were brightly painted, with pictures in frames. (I couldn't make out what was in the pictures much.) On the floor between the beds there was a pink and green rug.

I had muzzy memories of coming round from the anaesthetic, in some kind of hospital place, of Skinner's voice and Dr Franklin's voice, and being handled and answering questions . . . but everything was different now. This was like a normal hotel room.

Except that there were no windows.

We must have woken at almost the same moment. 'Hey,' said Miranda, sitting up. 'Am I dreaming?'

'We're both dreaming. Let's hope it lasts. My head aches horribly, does yours?'

'Yeah. That'll be from the general anaesthetic.'

We were wearing green hospital-type gowns, tied at the back with tapes. Oh, it was an amazing relief to have my arms free again. To be still me! I sat there gazing at these knobbly-elbowed, knobby-wristed, skinny arms of mine with great admiration, greeting the scratches and scabs from my castaway's life like old friends. My hands too, how wonderful!

'I've never realised,' I said, waving my arms about and wriggling my hands in front of my face, 'how much I *love* my hands.'

Then we looked at each other, and remembered—

We had not escaped. This 'hotel room' was a fake and a sham. We were still the prisoners of a cruel madman, and he'd already started doing horrible things to us.

Our chests hurt. We undid each other's tapes so we could see what had been done. We each had a square dressing on our chests, below the collarbones. The place was very sore and there was a bruise showing around the edges of the dressing.

Nothing else seemed to have happened.

'We won't talk about it,' said Miranda. 'Not yet. We'll give ourselves a break.'

So we put the horror out of our minds, as best we could. We got up and padded around, exploring our new territory together. There were three doors. The first one we tried led to a bathroom, with a shower, a basin and a toilet. There were big fluffy white towels on a heated rack, shower gel, nice soap, shampoo, conditioner, toothpaste and toothbrushes, hairbrushes, combs, everything.

Except no windows.

The second door led to a living room. There were two armchairs, covered in a pretty, blue-green patterned fabric, a coffee-table, more pictures on the walls, and a very fancy brand new combination tv and video. The shelf under the tv held a playstation and a library of video discs and games. There was a normal-looking kitchen fridge, that was humming very gently. There were no windows in here, either. There was a door that must lead to the outside world, but it was locked, of course.

We went back into our bedroom, opened the third door in there and found a walk-in closet full of clothes on hangers and shelves. They were in teenage sizes – shorts and teeshirts, jeans and dresses, underwear. American labels, all clean and new and good quality.

'Oh, yuk,' I said. 'Do you think he sent for these when he knew we were on the beach?' The thought of wearing clothes bought for me by Dr Franklin was hateful, and I said so. 'I don't want to wear these. I'd feel like an animal dressed up.'

'No,' said Miranda firmly. 'These aren't specially for us. Think about it. Dr Franklin's staff, the orderlies and technicians, have to have everything provided for them. They all live here, and they have families, Skinner said so. That'll be where the clothes come from. Dr Franklin's Island General Stores. Don't let little things get to you, Semi. Remember, quality of life.'

'Quality of life.'

So we dressed. We even laughed about it, as we sorted through our collection, looking for things that fitted. It was so long since we'd had a choice of clothes, we tried on practically everything in the closet before we were finished. We were extremely thin, and it seemed as if the island's resident teenagers were inclined to be on the large side of big, but with cinched-in belts and going for the sloppy, off-the-shoulder, beach-gypsy look, we managed to kit ourselves out to our satisfaction. When we'd picked out our clothes, we showered extravagantly with lots of scented foam, and washed our hair; and dressed. Then we looked in the fridge, and found a big platter of beautifully prepared tropical fruit, a tray of cold pastries, a pitcher of pinky-orange juice, and lots of bottled water.

'Okay,' said Miranda, when we'd carried this feast to our

coffee table, and sat looking at it, too thrilled to start eating. 'I've got an idea. Let's start the count again. Let's call this Day Forty-Two. We can't tell what time it is, but that meal looks like breakfast, so we'll call this the morning of Day Forty-Two.'

'Skinner said we'd been on the beach forty-five days.'

'I know he did, but this is *our* count.'

'But what are we going to do for notches? Scratch on the wall with our fingernails?'

There was nothing to write with, no paper, no books, and no knives or forks either.

'No, let's not do that. Let's keep the count in our heads, the way we did on the expeditions to the headlands. Then no one can take it away from us.' She looked up at the ceiling, significantly. I could not see any camera eyes peering down, but I knew at once what she meant. For a moment then, we sobered up. We thought about how everything we did was watched, everything we said was heard, and how our one chance of escape had failed. This time Miranda didn't order me to stay cheerful. She reached out her hand. I took it. We held hands tightly, staring at the empty screen of the tv.

Then we let go, and started eating our delicious breakfast, without another word.

We drank the juice out of the pitcher, because we hadn't found any cups.

Later that 'day' Dr Franklin came to see us, and explained how things would work. Now that our treatment had begun (that's what he called it), we would be free, in these rooms, as long as we behaved ourselves. No one but he and Dr Skinner would be involved in our 'treatment', but we would have to prove that we could be trusted with the people who provided our day to day care. When an orderly was bringing our meals, a red light would go on over the door. We were to go into our bedroom and stay there until another red light over the door in there went off. There'd be some 'unavoidable contact' with the staff, when the rooms had to be cleaned, or our laundry taken away and delivered back. We had to agree not to speak to them, or leave them messages, or make any attempt to communicate.

If there was any trouble, we'd be back in the straitjackets.

It went without saying, he'd have us under video surveillance all the time.

We said we'd co-operate.

I think this was the time when he made us say that I wanted to be a fish, and Miranda wanted to be a bird. But I'm not sure whether we'd already done that.

When he'd gone, I went into the bedroom and sat on my bed, my head in my hands. I didn't cry, I didn't feel like screaming. I felt as if I never wanted to move again. I wished I could simply stop breathing. Miranda came and sat down next to me.

'We're volunteers. So if it happens, we're glad we're having the treatment.'

'Leave me alone.'

'But it still might not happen. Semi, listen. We are not done yet. Until the last, last chance, the next thing we try might work. Say it?'

'The next thing we try might work,' I whispered. 'But it *won't*, Miranda.'

'We *don't know that*. We'll work on the guards, could be we'll get through to one of them. We'll look for the airconditioning vents, maybe we can escape through them. We may have a chance to get at Skinner again—'

'*He's* watching us now. He's hearing you say all this.'

'Maybe. Okay, probably. But he isn't finding out any secrets. He knows we want to escape. And *he doesn't know*, not for absolutely certain, that we won't find a way. Hey, look at us so far. We were in straitjackets, we thought we were done for. Next thing we know, we're here in this nice room. With tv and a fridge and everything. So, things can get better as well as worse. Come on, Semi. Cheer up.'

So we hugged, and I smiled, and I was better. I knew from the beach that it was no use trying to resist. Miranda wouldn't let you give up. Eventually the lights dimmed and the rooms went dark. We realised that this was our 'night'; and we went to bed.

On the second day, we had another operation.

For two days after that we kept trying to speak to the orderlies, and we chipped and poked at every corner of our rooms. Then Doctor Franklin told us that if we didn't stop this he'd put us back in straitjackets, keep us each under permanent restraint in solitary confinement, and feed us by tubes into our stomachs.

We knew he meant it, so we stopped.

He told us that there was no longer any sense in our trying to escape. We'd had our first infusion of artificial DNA. The thing was done. We were transgenics. When the changes in our cells reached critical levels, we were going to be completely helpless. We'd die if we weren't in his care. Of course we didn't believe him. We believed in the strait-jackets all right, but not the rest. Not deep down. We felt normal, we weren't visibly growing fins and wings. I was the one who panicked and Miranda was the one who kept calm, but we could neither of us really believe the truth. How could we?

When a human embyro begins to develop it's a little tight

cluster of cells, and each one of those cells has the potential to grow into any part of the human body. This power to change gets switched off when the baby starts growing, but in your bone marrow there are cells called stem cells, that are like the cells in that early state. Dr Franklin and Dr Skinner had removed samples of our bone marrow, and doctored some of the cells so they worked as much like our original embryonic stem cells (that's their full official name) as possible. Then he'd given us each an 'infusion' of the doctored cells, with the artificial DNA added. This 'rebuilt' DNA had been cut and spliced with new 'bird' genes for Miranda, and 'fish' genes for me. We'd have to have several of these infusions, he couldn't tell how many, depending on how well we responded.

Dr Franklin told us we mustn't think we were going to turn into a haddock and a robin! He'd used pieces of original animal genes as his basic material, but the final product, that had been injected into us, was *new* – genes that he'd created, that had never existed before in the world. He said we'd still be human, when the treatment was successfully completed, but *more than human*.

He came to visit us every day, took blood samples, tested our reflexes and things; and spent about an hour explaining what was supposed to happen, with fancy computer graphics and diagrams, which he showed us by plugging his computer into our fancy tv. Every time he came to see us we both had to do more of the IQ test things, but he talked to Miranda much more than he talked to me – about how wonderfully birds are adapted for flight, and how cleverly he, Dr Franklin, had fitted these adaptions into his artificial genes. How her skeleton would have to change. How big her wings would have to be, to get a human-sized 'bird' off the ground.

He hardly said anything to me about turning into a fish.

It should have been a relief that he didn't talk to me, but the weird thing was, I felt jealous. When Dr Franklin sat with Miranda, talking to her as if she was his favourite student, and complimenting her for asking good questions, I felt hurt and left out. When he looked at my medical test results and frowned, I felt as if I'd done something wrong.

'He's playing mind-games,' said Miranda, when we were alone. 'Remember what Skinner said. He doesn't just want to change us, he wants to "study the psychological effects". He's seeing how we react to being treated in different ways. Don't let it get to you.'

Yes, we knew there was probably always someone listening, and watching. We'd decided we didn't care. Next time we were working on an escape, that would be the time to worry about keeping secrets from our captors. We hadn't given up. The next thing we tried might work. We told each other (in whispers, last thing at night) that we'd better have a really good plan, because we'd only get one chance.

But we were so afraid of being put back in the straitjackets that we let the days go by.

The time passed strangely easily. We watched films, we played games, we did fashion shows for each other, we plucked each other's eyebrows and painted each other's nails. We found the plastic drinking glasses in the bathroom cabinet, and didn't have to drink out of the pitcher any more. We found the microwave, and warmed up our pastries in the morning, so they were lovely and soft and gooey. We didn't speak to the orderlies, but if we got anything to eat that we didn't like, we would mutilate it with toothpaste swirls and hair conditioner, to show our disapproval, and that kind of food would not turn up again.

(I developed a real aversion to seafood. Miranda would still eat chicken, though.)

And all the time, it was as if we'd been pushed off the top of a very, very high building: so high that we seemed to be floating. But we weren't floating, we were falling.

Sometimes I'd lie awake in our 'night' and imagine I could hear the jungle cat howling.

Sometimes in the 'day', when Dr Franklin would arrive with his laptop and his tests and his educational toys, I'd wish that I was chained up and blindfolded in some dark cellar. I'd rather have been like that than have to face his cold bright eyes. He was never nasty to us. Even when he was telling us off, and warning us about the straitjackets, he was polite. But I had the strange feeling he was pretending too. We were pretending we were his students, his volunteers, his willing guinea pigs. He was pretending that he thought we were human, because that was the way to get the best behaviour out of us. But in his mind, we were animals. So it didn't matter what he did to us.

But whenever I felt bad, Miranda was there. She'd talk about how we were going to escape, making up the most ridiculous plots. Or she'd talk about how amazing it would be when we had our superpowers, and how excited she was about being a volunteer. We'd lie on our beds describing how wonderful it would be, when she could fly and I could explore the beautiful oceans. I didn't believe her, of course; and I knew she didn't believe it either. We weren't going to escape, we weren't going to have magic powers. We were going to die, horribly. But as long as she kept talking like that I could pretend. I could go on being cheerful, hour by hour and day by day, instead of crouching in a corner howling.

Every day and every hour, I knew she was saving my life.

And when Miranda needed me, when she broke down and cried, I was there.

She wasn't always brave. She was just so much braver than me.

Every night, last thing before we turned away from each other to fall asleep, we'd cut the notch. It was important to keep counting the days, even though we knew we'd almost certainly lost track. It helped a lot. We'd pretend we were back on the beach, under our favourite palm tree. Then I'd say the notch was cut, or Miranda would say she was doing it; and we'd play the tomorrow game.

'Tomorrow,' I might say, 'there'll be muesli and cold fresh milk for breakfast.'

There was never any milk, except some Long Life stuff that tasted like dishwater, which we gave the toothpaste/conditioner treatment, and would not drink.

'Tomorrow,' Miranda might reply, 'the orderly will accidentally leave behind a toolbox with dynamite in it. We'll blast our way out, take over the labs, reverse our treatment, and zoom away from this stinking island in our dear Dr Franklin's private jet.'

'Do you know how to fly a jet plane?'

'Of course I do. I'm half-bird, you know. I can fly anything.'

But while the voices talked nonsense, the hands were clinging so tight it hurt, telling each other the truth. It was a special treat we allowed ourselves. For a few moments, every night, our hands could say what we mustn't ever say aloud – unless we wanted to start screaming.

We're so frightened, so terribly frightened.

Tomorrow the horror begins. Tomorrow we start turning into monsters.

Day Forty-Nine (or so.)

Miranda felt sick, and couldn't eat her breakfast. When Dr Franklin came he took the usual blood samples, put them in a little machine which he plugged into the tv, and looked at the results on the screen. He didn't seem pleased with mine. I felt bad about that. Then he gave us both something he said was a vitamin injection, and some pills we had to swallow. He put a patch, like one of those nicotine patches people wear when they are trying to stop smoking, on my upper arm. He told me not to take it off, because it was an immuno-suppressant, to boost the effect of the infusions. Miranda didn't get one.

Day Fifty-Five.

We never missed the notch cutting, not as long as we were together. If I leave out days it's because nothing happened: we were getting dressed and eating meals, playing games and watching films, going into the bedroom when the red light came on (we called it the fasten-seat-belts sign), and putting up with Dr Franklin's visit. On day Fifty-Five Miranda hadn't slept. I knew because I'd heard her tossing and turning all night. When we were eating breakfast, one of her back teeth fell out. It didn't hurt, there was no blood. It was the cap of a back tooth, the roots must have been re-absorbed into the gum.

'It doesn't mean anything,' she said. 'It's not serious. It's probably because of all that time on the beach, hardly eating anything.'

We played around with our clothes collection, but she kept going and looking at herself in the mirror in the bathroom, and coming back frowning. About lunchtime, but before the fasten-seat-belts light came on to warn us the orderly was coming, she came back from one of these trips and said, 'Semi, will you look at my chest?'

So I looked. Between her breasts, (we weren't wearing bras, there were none that remotely fitted our skinny chests), there was a sort of low ridge, that went upwards from her diaphragm towards her throat. The skin over it looked stretched, with little whiteish lines in it, and the whole bump was much paler than her tan. Our living room was littered with things Dr Franklin had brought with him to illustrate his lectures. There was a bird's skeleton mounted on a stand; there were feathers of various kinds lying on the coffee table. Miranda went over and looked at the skeleton, tracing the bones with her finger.

'My sternum must grow,' she murmured, in a strange, distant voice. 'The sternum, that's the breastbone, has to grow big enough to anchor the flight muscles. A bird's flight muscles are up to twenty per cent, that's a fifth, of its body weight. Think of it. Something big enough to carry those huge muscles will stick out of my chest like a keel underneath a boat.'

My mouth had gone dry. I couldn't speak.

'So this is it,' she said quietly, 'It's going to happen.'

She took hold of me by the shoulders, and stared at me with big, burning eyes. 'Exciting.' she said fiercely. 'An adventure. Repeat after me, Semi. An exciting adventure, a thrilling chance to have superpowers. You got that? *Say it.*'

'An exciting adventure,' I managed to mumble. I wiped my tears with my fingers. She laughed at me, and we hugged as well as we could, so's not to hurt her.

By the end of that day, four more of her back teeth had come out.

I still didn't have any symptoms at all.

Day Fifty-Six.
Dr Franklin says Miranda losing her teeth is fine, she'll be

perfectly okay after the transgenic effect is complete, and not to worry. Miranda says her bones hurt. All her joints, especially her wrists and elbows, look sore and swollen. We asked Dr Franklin for a supply of painkillers, but he says we can't have any 'self-administered' medicines; or any drugs to suppress the nausea, because it would interfere with the procedures. Maybe he thinks we'd try to kill ourselves.

If that's what he thinks, he might be right if it was only me. But he doesn't know Miranda. She's tougher than that. And while Miranda can keep going, I can.

We're still human. The next thing we try might work.

Day Fifty-Seven.
Miranda's breastbone is enlarging incredibly fast. I think it's getting bigger by the hour. She's stopped talking about being in pain, but I know it's hurting her. When Dr Franklin came today, he brought a freshly killed jungle pigeon, and spent ages talking to her about lift, and flight angles, and showing her how marvellously a bird's wing can change shape as it flies; how the tail spreads and twists, folds up and spreads out, like the tailplane of an aircraft, acting as a stabiliser and a rudder. Then he sat with her while she did another of his IQ tests. She has to use a keyboard, and work on the screen. Her finger joints are too sore for her to hold a pen.

I think her fingers are getting longer.

I didn't have to do an IQ test. I sat there stroking the pigeon. Its eyes were closed, its feathers were soft and downy, grey with a greeny-pink sheen. It reminded me of outdoors, of trees and sky and all sorts of things I probably wouldn't ever see again. I wished it didn't have to be dead. Dr Franklin kept glancing at me when he thought I wasn't looking. I suppose I looked a bit mad, sitting there petting a dead bird.

I know he thinks I'm the weak link. That's why he never tells me anything about being a fish. Either that, or there's nothing interesting to say. But I'm beginning to suspect that my infusions simply didn't work. Miranda will leave me, she'll go on the great adventure alone, and I'll be left behind.

When he left, he took the pigeon with him. I was sorry. I had wanted to keep it.

Miranda sat for a long while saying nothing, staring at the blank tv. She kept opening her mouth as if she was yawning, and touching the corners of her lips.

Finally she said, 'Do' mi 'oice 'ound staynge?'

I was frightened, so I said loudly, 'No! No it doesn't sound strange at all!'

'My mouth feels weird,' she said and we both smiled in relief, because that time she sounded normal. 'I think all my teeth are going to fall out,' she said coolly, as if this was the most ordinary thing in the world. 'Birds don't have teeth, do they? Maybe I have to have no teeth, or I won't be able to fly.'

'Ask Dr Franklin. He'll explain it to you.'

It's hard to describe how we felt about Dr Franklin. We were terrified of him and we didn't ever stop hating him, but we longed for his visits. I was jealous of the attention he paid to Miranda, but I also thought it was right, because she *was* more important than me, at least that's how I felt. She deserved more of his favour.

He was like a god.

People who get kidnapped, or who are held hostage by terrorists, often behave like this. They start depending on the kidnappers, and treating them with lots of crazy respect, because they have nowhere else to turn. We'd agreed we'd try to remember that the way we felt about him wasn't real, it was a survival trick our minds were playing. Miranda said, 'We can't stop what's happening to our bodies, but we *can* control what happens to our minds.' But it got harder.

We didn't have anyone else but Dr Franklin, all through this time. I suppose Skinner must have been involved in the things that were done to us when we were taken to the operating theatre (we were always unconcious for those trips); but we never saw him. I think he wasn't trusted to be near us, unless we were out cold, (not until it was obviously too late) in case we were able to convince him to help us.

I don't think the orderlies knew what was happening. As far as they were concerned we were trespassers, being kept away from the secret stuff, until Dr Franklin could arrange for us to be sent back where we came from. Or something like that. They never saw us after things started to get weird. Dr Franklin and Dr Skinner looked after us then pretty much entirely by themselves.

The technicians, the ones who brought us back when we tried to get away, and the ones who acted as nurses for the two doctors, *must* have known. I don't know what Dr Franklin told them, if he told them anything. Maybe he told them we were ill, and being given treatment that would save our lives, and we were crazy too, and that was why we had to be kept locked up. But whatever they knew, I suppose I can understand why they didn't try to help us. Dr Franklin was like a god to us. They probably felt the same way. He was a very impressive person.

Also, to be brutal, they had their families to think of. They knew about that ward with the cages round the beds. They knew enough to understand that the scientists needed *young* people for the human trials. If they thought it was a case of letting us be guinea pigs, or letting it happen to their own children, I suppose they didn't have much choice.

Day Fifty-Nine.
Miranda woke up and started searching around her pillow. I didn't know what she was doing, until she said, calmly, 'Oh, my front teeth. Look, they've started dropping out now. Here they are, lying on the pillow for the tooth fairy. He told me it might happen. Birds don't have teeth, do they?'

I nodded, bending over her and stroking her black hair back from her sunken face.

'I think he must be giving me tranquillisers, Semi. Everything seems so far away.'

I could hardly make out what she was saying, but I didn't bother telling her that. She knew. Her eyes were getting bigger, or else her face was getting smaller . . . the bone shifting into a different pattern. Her cheekbones and her jaws were changing shape.

I was still taking my share of the daily injections, the patches and the pills: but I still had no symptoms. I couldn't breathe at night, and I was rather floppy. But that didn't have to be anything to do with the treatment. It was stuffy in these windowless rooms, in spite of the aircon; and neither of us was eating much. We had no appetite. I told Miranda to stay in bed, and went to the bathroom, because for the first time I felt something odd.

When I looked in the mirror, I saw marks like bruises on my neck. When I touched them, the skin came apart under my fingertips. It was as if two rows of little wounds had opened in my throat, from the inside: but there was no blood. I was glad of that. I've always been a coward about the sight of blood. I put my hands over my chest, wondering what was happening to my lungs, inside there, changing so that I could breathe under water.

Big deal.

I'd chosen the easy option, and I wished desperately that I could have my choice back, and save Miranda from her cruel tortures. But it was too late.

Dr Franklin didn't stay long, when he came that morning. There'd be no more lessons on the science of flight now, no more IQ tests for Miranda. Later he came back with Dr Skinner. They set up the equipment Miranda needed, to get her through the critical stages of her change. I didn't speak to Skinner. I could hardly bear to look at him. I had to keep going into the bathroom. I couldn't stop crying, because she was leaving me, she was going somewhere I couldn't follow. But I managed to stay cheerful when I was by her.

'Exciting,' I whispered, holding her hand gently. 'A tremendous challenge. You're going to have superpowers.'

Day Sixty-Two.
Miranda complained that there was something wrong with her shoulders. She said, 'I can't get my arms to come forwards, it's as if both my shoulders are dislocated.' I'd been having to help her a lot, almost carrying her to the bathroom when she needed to go. It wasn't hard, she was so light, it felt as if she was made of paper. But I couldn't do that anymore, since the drip had been put into her stomach, and the monitor machines had been taped to her chest and head.

I moved the stand that was carrying the drip-feed. She wasn't able to form words well, but I knew she wanted me to have a look. I turned back the sheet and saw red smudges on her pyjama jacket. My hands were clumsy. I didn't have much feeling in them, due to the immuno-suppressants or something. When I'd managed to unfasten the buttons, I saw that the keel of her breastbone had burst through the skin, and the raw flesh was oozing blood and clear fluid. I could see the bone, all white, and the thick bands of gleaming purply red, which were the new muscles—

'What does it look like?' she asked.

I could barely understand her. 'It looks like you're growing wings,' I said, swallowing back tears, and I smiled at her. 'It looks like you'll soon, *soon* be able to fly—'

'Love to be able to fly,' said Miranda, 'oh, *love* to be able to fly.'

I buzzed for Dr Franklin.

They both came. 'What's happening to her?' I begged. 'Is this supposed to happen?' I was sure she was dying. Nobody could live with their chest split open like that.

Dr Franklin said, 'Please keep calm, Semi. You're disturbing Miranda.'

But I could see that even the mad scientist was alarmed. 'You don't know, do you?' I cried, horrified. 'You *don't know*! You had no idea what your treatment would do to us!'

On Day Sixy-Three I couldn't hold her hand any more, because she didn't have any hands.

Day Sixty-Four.
They took Miranda away. They took the whole bed, they couldn't have lifted her out of it, she was too twisted-up and fragile. All I could see of her that was still Miranda, was her eyes.

'Exciting,' I whispered, as they wheeled her out. 'Great adventure. You first, me soon—'

'Tomorrow,' she gasped, struggling with her twisted mouth, 'Fly away.'

I thought I would never see her again.

Day Sixty-Five.
Miranda's gone. I'm alone.

Tomorrow I'm going to be so big and strong. I'll bust these walls down. I'll come and find you, Miranda, and let you out of your cage. You'll pick me up in your beak, we'll fly away.

I couldn't make myself get up, the morning that she wasn't there. I lay there telling myself that I was lying still because I wanted to lie still. I didn't want to let Miranda down, so I stayed calm. I went to live in my head again. It was nice and peaceful.

I think Day Sixty-Four was probably the last time I got up, but I'm not sure. I know it was from Day Sixty-Five that I absolutely couldn't make my arms and legs obey me. On Day Sixty-Seven I woke up and found that my arms . . . didn't seem to belong to me any more. That was weird. I could lift my head, barely, and see them lying there on either side of me. They looked like bits of old wood. I couldn't move them, but it didn't worry me. I had no feeling for them at all. My mind had sort of dumped them, like rubbish.

Something strange was happening to my legs too, but it was so much effort to breathe that I couldn't worry about it. And everything hurt.

I thought, *oh, I didn't get the easy option after all,* and I was glad.

I wasn't awake, I wasn't asleep, I wasn't unconscious. I was in some state that was none of those things. Sometimes I glimpsed Dr Franklin's face, swimming into focus out of the mists. Occasionally I heard Skinner's voice, in the background. Sometimes I felt hands lifting me, rearranging me, giving me injections (it didn't hurt when the needle went in). My skin's getting thicker, I thought. Maybe I'm growing scales and fins now . . . and I fell into a long dream, a long *flowing* dream, where the covers and the bed had disappeared, and I didn't know who I was, or where I was, or what I was.

Time didn't pass any more, it flowed.

I went through the change and came out the other side. They moved me, as soon as they possibly could, to an indoor tank (you can't keep a fish-monster-mutant alive in an intensive care bed). Later on, glimpses of the days I spent in that tank came back to me, but while it was happening I wasn't really aware of anything. I was adapting, my brain making new connections, my new senses plugging in and testing themselves. I had the vague idea that Skinner and Dr Franklin were trying to find out what was going on inside my head, measuring my brainwaves with a sort of cap of wires . . . and a vague idea that I didn't perform very well. But when I next woke up properly, all that stuff was gone from my mind. Thinking about any of it was like trying to remember a forgotten nightmare.

Everything was different, utterly different.

Day Seventy-Eight.

I woke out of a deep sleep, feeling fine. The first thing I thought, before I opened my eyes, was *what day is this?* I knew there'd been a gap. I didn't want to let Miranda down, the count was so important. I 'lay there' without even thinking whether I was in a bed or where I was, trying to work it out. In the end I calculated this must be about the seventy-eighth day. Anyway, that's what I decided to call it. So, here I am I thought. Seventy-Eight days from Miami airport, and what a lot of things had happened to me since then!

I've been in a plane crash.

I've swum through a lagoon full of sharks.

I've survived on a beach, made fire, climbed for coconuts, built a house, speared a fish.

Almost hunted a pig, once—

And I'm still alive!

I felt so calm and happy. This didn't strike me as strange. It seemed the normal way to feel. At last, I opened my eyes. The first tremendous shock was that I could see, perfectly. The world didn't look anything like the blurred world I'd been used to seeing since the plane crash – the same blurred world that I'd lived with all my life, whenever I didn't have my contact lenses in or my glasses on. I could tell I was seeing things from a different angle, to say the least. But everything was the way it was supposed to be. There was nothing missing, no lost details, nothing faulty.

The second, tremendous shock I got was that my arms had turned into wings.

I thought, *what*? But I was supposed to turn into a fish!

I waved my arms up and down. They flowed around me in a smooth, wide delta shape, and I realised there was an even bigger change (apart from the fact that I had no hands, which didn't bother me). The stick-figure Semi that I used to imagine – normally living in my heart but able to move into my head when things got tough – had gone, or changed tremendously. My head wasn't separate from my body any more. My head and my heart were together, in the centre of me, and *me* was this smooth, flowing, delta-plane.

I gave a kind of start, and a jump . . . which is when I

realised that my legs weren't dangling extra things anymore, they were *inside me* as well. When I 'kicked' (the word belonged to that old stick-figure Semi, it was no use any more, I'd have to think of other words), my whole body responded. I went flying forwards, backwards, up, down, with perfect control, any direction I wanted. I was free, so free.

If waking up in a straitjacket was bad, then this freedom, was like . . . How can I describe it? It was as if being normal had been a straitjacket, and this was how it felt when all the horrible restraints, that you'd been suffering all your life without realising it, were magically taken away.

It was beautiful. I was flying.

Oh, Miranda. This is brilliant! It really is a great adventure!

And I can fly! I've turned into a bird as well!

I don't know what kind of bird I thought I'd been turned into, a delta-shaped bird with a body in the form of one smooth wing. There's no such thing.

Maybe I thought I'd been transformed into a teenager-sized Stealth bomber.

I had called out to Miranda without thinking. It had felt like shouting – though, as if in a dream, I knew I wasn't making any sound. But when I 'shouted' like that, something happened. It was as if I finally woke up, finally came out of dreamland.

I was floating in water. It was over me, under me, all around me. It was the air that I breathed. I wasn't frightened. I still felt good, and delighted with my new body. Sunlight was warming my back, and that felt very nice. I glided up towards the shimmering liquid light, until I was breaking the surface, and looked around.

There was a problem for a moment with my new eyes,

which were getting the picture in an altered format. I had to flip some mental switches to sort it into human terms, like wide-screen tv being squeezed onto a square screen. But it wasn't difficult. I saw that I was in a big pool, swimming-pool sized, in an enclosure with trees and bushes and bright coloured flowers. I could see a fence, that stretched up and went over my pool. High above, I could see a dark mesh against the blue sky. For a moment I thought (still feeling calm and cheerful), for heaven's sake, there's no need for that! I'm not going to fly away!

. . and then I felt a shadow. I looked up, and saw a great bird-shape gliding over my pool, with dark wings outspread, the flight feathers parted, fingering the air. The shadow left me as the creature banked and dived. I heard a thump, and the water rumbled with vibration. A thing like a big dark bird, big as an eagle, black as a raven, was standing by the edge of my pool. Its folded wings were covered in glossy feathers. The rest of its body was covered in a short pelt of shining black hair. Its legs were scaled and leathery like a bird's, but jointed like human legs. Its feet were scaled like a bird's, but its five powerful clawed toes looked as if they were built like human fingers. Its head was very birdlike, the great eyes set on either side, of a nose and mouth that had fused into a single red beak. But the base of this beak was wide, like a fledgling's beak; and it had an expression. The bird was smiling.

Oh God, I thought. *It's Miranda!*

She turned her head to look at me, the way birds do, one eye at a time. Then she croaked, and hopped, and croaked again . . .

Miranda!

I had no voice, I couldn't speak. Neither could she.

She was in the air, I was in the water.

We were alive. We'd survived. But we were parted forever.

If Miranda had realised this would happen, she'd never told me. It had never come into our imagining and pretending. I hadn't thought about it at all. I'd been so sure that we were going to die, the problem of her being a bird and me a fish had never once crossed my mind. The shock was too much. I stared at Miranda, and everything that had delighted me about my new form turned to horror. I wasn't a girl any more. I was a monster. My arms, my legs . . . gone! No voice, no hands, a nightmare come true. I tried to scream.

Of course, I *couldn't* scream. I blacked out instead.

8

Next thing I knew, everything was white. It was like being inside a cloud: like being surrounded by the dazzling, soft, white cloud-country you sometimes see from a plane window. I saw Miranda, standing with her back to me. I knew it was Miranda at once, Miranda the way I remembered her from the beach. But there was something wrong. She seemed smaller, her shoulders looked narrower and they were hunched forward as if she was trying to hide. Her legs didn't look so long, and even her hair looked less thick and shiny. She turned around, and smiled at me, with a timid, anxious expression. I tried to speak. I think I managed to say her name. I looked down at myself. I saw a human body, I saw my hands, my clothes. But Miranda was not like Miranda, and I knew I couldn't be human. I panicked. Everything started to shake. The whiteness went away into a kind of greyed-out dark.

I could hear someone calling me. Miranda was calling my name, over and over. I tried to answer, I couldn't . . .

. . . and then I could.

My voice came out in a whimper, and then a loud wail. I couldn't control it . . .

. . . and then I could.

Then I was in the white place again. Miranda was standing there, hugging her arms around herself. We were dressed in our beach clothes. She still looked *strange*. A Miranda with all the strength and confidence drained out of her.

'What's happening?' I pleaded. 'Oh, Miranda, what is this place? Are we dead?'

I'd had a horrible idea. Maybe this strange white place was . . . was heaven?

'I don't think we're dead,' said Miranda, sounding very unsure. 'I think we're alive in the . . . the other place, the cage. I think this is radio telepathy.'

'*Radio telepathy*?' I repeated, helplessly. 'What's that?'

I tried looking around, but . . . that didn't work. Everywhere you actually *looked* at the whiteness, it blurred out, and vanished into nothingness. The effect made me feel as if I was going to be sick. I realised I'd better concentrate on looking at Miranda.

'It's something else they did to us, Semi. Doctor Franklin told me, when he'd taken me away from the hotel room for the last bit of the change. They put microchips in our brains, little tiny radios connected to our speech centres, so that we can talk to each other although we have animal bodies.'

'Nobody told me that!' (I felt jealous. As usual, Miranda had been given more information, and treated better than me.)

'Maybe they did but you don't remember. You've been here in . . . the cage . . . for a day and a night. I've been calling and calling to you, and you didn't answer. Oh God, I thought they'd made you into a dumb animal. I thought I would be all alone.'

'But what's this *white stuff*?'

She shook her head. 'I don't know. This isn't what they told me. They put you in the pool yesterday. I called and

112

called to you, in my head, the way I remembered Dr Franklin telling me I would be able to. But you didn't answer. I kept trying for hours, and you still didn't answer. I thought that you were a dumb animal. I thought they'd destroyed your brain . . . Then I heard you call my name, and suddenly I was here. I saw you, but you fell apart, and then you came back together again . . . I'm not explaining this well.'

Both of us sat down. The whiteness under us stayed solid; it behaved like ground. We didn't try to touch each other, not yet. I thought I would go crazy if I touched her and my hand went right through. I had the weirdest feeling of being in two places at once. I knew that while I sat with Miranda here, the mutant-fish monster that was also me was still swimming around in that pool.

'Well,' said Miranda at last. 'It seems like we survived.'

I nodded. 'Do you think he meant us to turn out like . . . the way we are?'

She shuddered. 'I don't think so. Remember what Dr Skinner said? Transgenic experiments can be random. I don't think they knew *how* we would turn out. That's the whole point of being a scientist, isn't it? You try things, to see what happens . . . I hate to break it to you, but we're in the zoo, Semi. When I fly up into the roof, I can see the whole compound. The courtyard next door to ours is where the other pathetic freaks are kept. That's where we are. In the freak zoo.'

We'd been supposed to change into a girl who could fly, and a girl who could breathe water. Instead we'd joined the capybara with the human legs, the octopus with a monkey's head, the wild piglet with human hands . . . the howling jungle cat.

Miranda crouched over, with her head in her hands. She

started rocking to and fro. I could see that she was shaking all over. I could hear her muttering '*freaks, freaks, freaks*—'

I'd seen Miranda in tears, but I'd never seen her like this. It frightened me horribly. It made me feel as if I was falling apart. *Miranda!* I cried, and my voice didn't sound real. Nothing here was real. Reality was two monsters in a cage, separated forever by more than bars, by more than locks and keys. I fought the terror down. I tried to remember what Miranda used to do, when I started to panic.

Talk to her, talk to her. Say anything, believe anything that makes things better—

'Hey, Miranda. Miranda! *Flight!* Think about flight! Think about how wonderful it is, the way birds can fly. Think about a feather, how it has to be built, the amazing way the filaments hook into each other to make a plane surface. Think about an . . . an aerofoil. How it has to be shaped, longer on the top than on the bottom, so the . . . the air resistance that's pushing it up ends up more than the air resistance that's pushing it down . . . The last thing you said to me was *love to be able to fly.*'

I was babbling, trying to remember Dr Franklin's lectures. 'Miranda, *please!*'

I think it was the desperation in my voice that reached her.

Somehow we were holding hands, and (thank goodness) it felt real.

'Love to be able to fly,' said Miranda, and laughed shakily.

'Are you okay?'

'I'm okay. I'm better. It's just . . . I was alone, and I thought you were a dumb animal.'

She said she was okay, but she still looked weak and timid. It was horrible of me, but I felt *angry* with her. How could she betray me like this? I needed Miranda to be strong! I wanted to yell at her, *you can't do this to me!*

Miranda let go of my hands. 'Semi, what is it? You . . . you're frightening me!'

'Me? Frightening? You're *kidding.* It's you that's behaving strangely. What's wrong with you? You were always so cool, so brave. You seem like a different person.'

I scowled at the timid, anxious girl I didn't seem to know. I saw in her cringing eyes the Semi that she saw, and I realised *she could see* my fury at being let down. My deep, secret envy of the person I had thought Miranda was—

We stared at each other for a long moment.

'Oh,' said Miranda at last. 'I think I get it—'

'Yeah. Me too. It's the telepathy.'

I looked at her, and I saw a girl who had to be best, because she was afraid she could never measure up to what was expected of her, no matter how hard she tried.

She looked at me, and saw the shy nerd who was always secretly angry with the people who found making friends easy. A person I didn't like very much. The real me.

'This is the real Miranda,' she said. 'This is the way I am inside. I'm not really strong and confident. I pretend. All the time you were relying on me, you and Arnie and then you alone, I was scared to death. I had to keep up a front, but that's all it was. A big pretence.'

'Maybe I'm not really shy. Maybe I just *don't like* people. I think I'm horrible.'

'Don't be stupid. You're the best friend I ever had. I always knew you were the strong one, inside,' said Miranda. 'Now I can see it, that's all.'

'If you were always scared to death and never showed it,' I said, 'you're even braver than I thought.'

Miranda let go of my hand, and pushed back her hair, and

she seemed like my Miranda again. Only more . . . even more my friend.

'You know what,' she said, with a wry grin. 'It really is wonderful to be able to fly.'

I nodded. 'This may sound weird, but it's wonderful to be a fish, too.'

'And we have this telepathy stuff. That's another good thing. But we'll have to learn to handle it better.'

'Yeah,' I agreed. It's not totally a good thing, to be able to see through *all* your friend's defences. Or to have her see through all your illusions about yourself, either. 'They didn't tell you how to work it at all?'

'If they did, I don't remember. All I remember is Dr Franklin saying we'd be free to talk to each other. They wouldn't be able to listen in.'

I laughed, and Miranda nodded. 'Another lie,' I said. 'I bet they're listening now.'

We sat there in silence, in the middle of our white cloud, thinking of our terrible, unbelievable, horrible situation. 'Maybe it's not so bad,' whispered Miranda. 'Maybe it's going to be okay. Remember what he said, when he used to come to the fake hotel room? About interplanetary travel? Remember he said that you could be an ambassador to a world where there was only ocean. And I could be sent to a planet where the sentient beings could fly, and we'd be able to deal with the aliens on their own terms? What if that's going to happen? What if he knows about a secret space programme, and we're the astronauts? I mean, I know it sounds impossible. But he's done other impossible things.'

I felt so sorry for her. She was talking the way she used to talk, to keep me going, to keep me from crawling into a corner, screaming. But that time was over now. Here in the white place, I could hear that she was trying to convince

116

herself, inventing a pitiful fantasy as much for her own sake as for mine. Poor Miranda.

'I don't want to visit another planet,' I said. 'I don't care if it's impossible or not. I don't care if Dr Franklin has built his own private spaceship. I just want to go home.'

It may sound ridiculous, seeing as I'd been turned into a monster, but that was what I still wanted. I thought of my brother coming down to the edge of the sea, and . . . patting me on my big slimy back. Or something. The idea brought tears to my imaginary human eyes; but it brought real hope as well. *I was still alive.* If we could escape from this evil genius and his horrible island, I could at least go home.

'Well, yeah,' said Miranda, slowly. 'Of course. We're still going to try and escape. We're never going to give up. Never.'

We looked at each other.

Miranda didn't say it, but it was as if her thought came straight into my mind.

If she could get out of the cage, she could fly away. Not me. I was stuck. I couldn't get to the sea. A fish can't climb fences, a fish can't tunnel through a mountainside.

I felt very stupid, for not having realised this before.

'I've had enough radio telepathy for now,' I said, after another silence. 'Do you know how to turn it off?'

'I suppose we'll have to try and find out.'

It was like adjusting to my new vision. I flipped some mental switches, trying to find the right ones. Miranda's face grew blurred. She faded out.

And we were gone. I to the water, she to the air.

Day Eighty (approximately!).

We found out how to use the radio telepathy, after a few tries. We discovered that if we tried too hard, (like mental shouting) we would end up in the white place. If we kept calm we could talk to each other. It was like calling someone on the phone. We'd say each other's names, in our minds, and it worked like dialling a number. When we'd learned how to do that, I told Miranda about waking up and calculating that it was Day Seventy-Eight. She thought that was hilarious. It was the first time I'd heard her really laugh in ages. But we don't care. It's our count, nobody else's. What does it matter how wrong we are?

Having human bodies in the white place is a bit too strange. But we've decided to meet there together last thing at night, the same as always, and we've started the imaginary notch-cutting ceremony again. So now it is Day Eighty.

One very good thing is that we don't have to make any effort to be our animal selves. Miranda-the-bird and Semi-the-fish know everything they need to know. They eat, sleep, move, react like the animals they are. All we have to do is learn to sort of keep our human thoughts out of the way, and everything just happens. Miranda says it's like having dual nationality. You're officially two people, but you don't feel anything odd.

In ways I'm more like a normal fish than Miranda is like a normal bird. I don't have any human limbs. I know what I look like, because Miranda has described me to me: plus I can see my shape, in the shadow that glides under me through the water. I look more or less like a manta-ray, the creature they call a devil-fish. Real manta-rays can get to be six metres or more across. They're non-violent, but if they are badly provoked, they can leap out of the ocean and even crush a small fishing boat. Or so legend says, in the Caribbean. I'm not as big as that. I wish I was. Then I wish Dr Franklin would come in here for a swim. I would leap on him and crush him against the tiles. But I'm only a ray fish the size of a flattened teenager.

My back is dark blue, with a sheen like shot silk. My underside is pearly white. I have a body that stretches smoothly out into two pectoral fins like wings, a tail that I can lash and splash in a very satisfying manner when I'm on the surface, eyes up at the front, and a wide mouth that filters plankton from the sunlit water of my pool. Oh, and I have two flippers at the base of my tail, on the underside of me, which must once have been my feet; but I don't use them much. I don't like them. They feel fidgety and strange, like rather useless people hanging around looking for a job, but there's nothing for them to do.

My pool is four metres deep, all over. (The fish-Semi can judge distances very precisely. I don't know how, she just can: and then the girl-Semi can translate what the fish-Semi knows, into metres and so on; it's one of those dual nationality things). There is a viewing window in a sunken passage at one end, where humans (such as the orderly who pours live plankton into the pool for me to eat) can stand and watch me swimming about. I don't like being watched, but fortunately I don't want to go down to that level much. I'm not a bottom-living fish. I like the sunlit water. And of course, I like to stay near Miranda. We don't talk to each other on our mental radio as much as you'd think. When we were in the fake hotel room, we used to ignore the fact that Dr Franklin had us under surveillance. We feel different about that now. Maybe it's because we're so much more helpless. But at least we can see each other, and be company for each other.

We're no longer human.

We're no longer part of an experiment, even an evil, crazy experiment.

We're failed leftovers, like the rest of the animals in Dr Franklin's zoo.

But it isn't entirely horrible. The other good thing about being changed, besides not having to learn how to swim and eat and so on, is that *our minds have been changed too.* The honest truth is, the fish-Semi part of me would be completely happy swimming, and measuring things, and thinking long, deep, dreamy sunlit thoughts . . . if it wasn't that I was stuck in this rotten little tiny pool. I know Miranda feels the same. She loves being a bird, she hates being a bird in a cage. It's strange. Before the change, we'd have thought that losing our human feelings, becoming mutant-monsters in our *minds* would have been the worst horror imaginable. In fact it turns out to be the only thing that makes life possible. The pain of loss, the pain of being parted from our families, is something we've had to live with for a long time: and it's still there. But there's no disgust and horror at being monsters. It isn't even so bad not being able to talk together. Often when we were castaways, we'd spend hours together each doing our separate things, hardly saying a word. We do the same in our enclosure.

What do animals do with themselves all day? A lot of nothing, basically.

Miranda hops and flaps around in the trees and bushes that grow in the border round my pool, plays about with twigs and flowers, and eats the fruit and stuff the orderly leaves for her. Or she flies up and down in the open air above the branches; or she perches in the roof and spies out over the compound. I glide around, I swim up and down, I filter plankton (so far, the strangest thing about being a fish: eating is like breathing. I don't feel as if I'm *doing* anything). I float on the surface, feeling the sun.

I have the strangest feeling that we could live like this, and be fairly content.

If only we weren't prisoners.

Sometimes, I accidentally do something that makes me feel how strong I really am, and how fast I could really move, and it's amazing.

I think, *no wonder I nearly died, turning into this amazing creature!*

But we are prisoners.

Every day the orderlies bring food, clear the remains of yesterday's food, and skim the pool. They're careful, but they have to open the gate to the enclosure. It's big enough for Miranda to run through, though nothing like wide enough for her to spread her wings.

She never tries it.

We haven't talked about the fact that Miranda can get away but I can't. There's no need to spell it out. I know she knows.

The plan would have to be that she leaves, and somehow fetches help.

Somehow.

Day Eighty-Two.

Today Dr Franklin finally came to visit. He turned up about halfway through the morning. I was floating in the middle of the pool, dreaming, when I was warned by Miranda, who came zooming down from the peak of the steel-mesh roof. She croaked loudly in her harsh bird-voice, and in my head I heard her say, *Semi! Watch out, here comes the boss.*

My eyes are at the front of my . . . my *me*, my delta-shape. I glided over to the side, watching as if from the periscope of a submarine. In my mind I flipped the switches

121

that had to be switched, to translate the foreshortened fish-me view of the enclosure fence, into a human-type image. I watched carefully as Dr Franklin came up to the gate. I was hoping I'd glimpse the keys he pressed on the lockpad. I hadn't managed to do that when the orderly came in, not yet. If we could get to know the combination, Miranda could easily make keystrokes with her beak, and have that gate open. Which wouldn't do me much good, but at least she would be free.

Dr Franklin didn't open the gate. He was carrying a folding chair. He unfolded it, about halfway along the fence, sat down, and took what looked like a mobile phone from his pocket. Both of us came and watched him: me in the water, Miranda pacing on the tiles by the side of the pool. She held her birdlike head on one side, one fierce eye fixed on me, and one on the mad scientist.

'Welcome to your new world,' he said. 'Miranda, Semi.' He settled his floppy sunhat more securely on his thick grey hair, and stared at us greedily. 'Amazing,' he muttered. 'Amazing!' An incredibly smug expression spread over his face. 'A truly extraordinary breakthrough. One day the world will share my triumph. One day, I will be able to reveal what I have achieved! But in the meantime—' he added, with a horrible smirk, 'there is much that can be done. Much that can be learned, from these two first successes.'

Miranda shrieked. I lifted my tail, and splashed it hard on the top of the water.

We were saying: *What do you mean successes? You've turned us into monsters, not superhumans. Now what are you going to do? Keep us locked up here forever?*

Dr Franklin shifted his chair, cleared his throat, and settled a little further back from the fence. 'I wonder how much you can still understand of normal human speech. It's rather difficult to tell. But I know you have discovered your radio telepathy. I know that you are making use of it! Neither of you ever asked me how you would be able to communicate in your transgenic forms. You never did show much curiosity, not even you, Miranda, my star pupil. I was surprised at that. How will humans who have been altered so much that they cannot talk, be able to work together? How will they be able to *stay human*? You didn't even think of that, apparently. But I had identified the problem, and I have solved it!'

I was amazed that he had the nerve to come and chat to us like this, after locking us up, putting us in straitjackets, turning us into monsters. Of course he was mad. But I suppose this is also the way normal people treat normal animals, a lot of the time. We keep zoo animals in cages, we keep dogs and horses as servants, we keep cows and pigs and sheep to kill and eat: and yet we somehow expect them to *like* us.

'Yes,' Dr Franklin went on, happily, 'I have made you telepathic. Yet another dream of humanity, that I have caused to come true. You are very highly privileged. You have left me far behind. I envy your powers, tremendously!'

Huh, I thought, bitterly. *You* haven't got a microchip in your brain. You haven't been turned into a monster. You stayed human, and you treated us like guinea pigs.

He stared at us. We stared back, like dumb animals. 'I wonder what's really going on in those heads,' he muttered. 'Difficult to say, difficult to say. There is certainly human brain activity, but the animal traits are very strong. Perhaps too strong.' For a moment he looked worried. Then he perked up. 'But that's good! I will be testing pyschological survival in extreme conditions. Which is exactly what I planned to do.'

Miranda spread her wings, and flew up into the branches of a tree.

Dr Franklin stopped talking, and gazed at her in wonder. 'Amazing,' he muttered again. 'Amazing! I have created flight!' He sounded so pleased with himself, and so completely oblivious of what he'd done to *us*, I seriously wanted to kill him.

'Well, well. You both seem to have adapted excellently, so far. Physically you are in very good shape, psychologically . . . hmm. We shall see. Now for the next phase of the experiment. In a few days, I am going to open the aviary. You'll be able to fly free, Miranda.'

Miranda shrieked.

It was a yell of surprise. I don't think she even meant to startle him. But Dr Franklin jumped up, clutching at his hat. The chair jerked backwards and tipped over.

I saw the expression on his face. He looked *scared*.

In a flash, I saw Miranda the way she must look to a human being. A great birdlike creature with human limbs, beautiful but nightmarish. Big as an eagle, with wings that could break your arm at a stroke, a hooked beak, strong taloned feet as dextrous as human hands. I'd seen the orderly being very careful about opening the enclosure gate. I'd thought it was to be sure she didn't get out. *He* was probably scared too. For a moment I felt pleased. Good, I thought. Serves them all right. But that was a stupid reaction. Dr Skinner had been afraid of us from the start, because we made him feel so guilty. It hadn't done us any good. They're afraid because we are monsters; I thought. Even the man who made us thinks we are monsters; and I didn't dare to look at Miranda, in case she was thinking the same thing.

'You'll be ringed and tagged, of course,' the scientist went on, having recovered his nerve. 'If you try to fly out of the valley you'll get a shock. If you persist, or if you interfere with my staff in any way, you will get a stronger shock, enough to stun you and render you unable to fly. We'll have to come out and find you and pick you up. Other than that, you'll be free to do as you please. What will happen, I wonder? Will you stay with your friend, who cannot leave her pool? Or will your animal instincts take over, and will you fly away and become a strange new part of this island's wildlife? We shall see, we shall see . . . I believe that there are still two human minds in there. What I want to know is whether your strong friendship, together with the internal radio link I have given you, will enable you to *remain* human, in this challenging situation. I will be observing your behaviour carefully. You supported each other on the beach, and through your treatment, most remarkably. Let's see if you can hold on to your humanity now.'

He stood up, and folded his chair. 'That's the vital question. Perhaps you will fail, you will fall by the wayside, and become no more than the couple of exotic animals that you appear. It matters little. I count this first trial a major success, even if it goes no further. Yes, almost more successful than I had dared to hope! Already, you have served the future of the race, Semi and Miranda. You should be very proud.'

Miranda shrieked again, and launched herself into the air. She swept into the roof of our big cage with one beat of her powerful wings, and went hurtling to and fro, from one end of the enclosure to the other, crying wildly. Dr Franklin stood staring at her. His mouth had dropped open. For a moment he almost looked horrified, as if even he couldn't quite believe what he had done to the teenage girl Miranda used to be. His star pupil. Then he frowned and shook his head, and hurried away, clutching his hat with one hand, his chair with the other.

9

On Day Eighty-Three, Dr Franklin came to the enclosure with two orderlies. The uniformed men came into the cage, armed with long metal rods and a big net. They threw the net over Miranda, and held her down. Then Dr Franklin came into the cage, wearing heavy gloves, reached through the net and fitted a black rubbery ring like a thick watchstrap on her leg. There was no need to throw the net over Miranda, or poke her with those rods. She wasn't doing anything, she didn't try to resist. But the men behaved as if she was simply a dangerous animal, and he did nothing to stop them. He treated her the same way. It was horrible to watch, it made me feel sick.

But after it was done, the men went off and came back with a mobile crane. They unfastened a big section of the steel mesh roof, and Miranda flew free.

On Day Eighty-Five, I found the sluice covers at the bottom of my pool.

I'd realised, after swimming around in it for a while, that my water was genuine seawater – not fake, salt-water aquarium substitute. Semi-the-girl wouldn't have known the difference, but Semi-the-fish couldn't be fooled about things like that. In my dual-nationality mind, it was as if I *remembered* everything that a natural-born tropical manta-ray would know. Only better than remembering, because this wasn't like Semi-the-girl remembering facts she'd learned, and sometimes getting them wrong. It was certain knowledge, like knowing the difference between light and dark. These 'memories' must come from the fish-DNA that had been grafted into my human DNA. But because I was girl as well as fish, I could think about my inbuilt animal knowledge with a human mind. I really enjoyed that.

The cover was a round flap of metal, set thirty centimetres above the floor of the pool. It was eighty-four centimetres across, as wide as the front section of my delta body; and painted turquoise, like the plastic-coated concrete of the wall. Water lapped through a set of ridged gaps out into a pipe, or tunnel, on the other side. There was another, smaller cover on the opposite wall, with water flowing from it *into* the pool. How interesting!

I think animals without hands have different minds from animals with hands. Animals with 'hands' that they can use to pick things up – like monkeys, humans, birds, mice, rats – tend to like being busy, and tinkering with things. Animals without 'hands', like snakes, or fish, or cats, are happy doing nothing for long periods. I'd always been a thoughtful person. As a fish, I completely shared the daydreamer-animal attitude to life. I had spent hours thinking about the real seawater, and what that must mean. Wondering about pipes and pumps. Having ideas about passages and tunnels in volcanic rock, like the passage we'd used to get into the hidden valley. Pondering on Dr Franklin's plans.

I hadn't felt as if the problem was urgent. My meaning-of-the-seawater ideas had drifted without any pressure, weaving in and out of other long, dreamy thoughts.

Now, looking at the sluice cover, my mind suddenly

speeded up. Fresh seawater was being pumped up from the ocean, and flowing through my pool. That wasn't so strange. Dr Franklin was very rich, and he'd told us he'd been planning to create a human fish, as one of his first human transgenics. The pool had to be in this hidden valley, so he'd had to have a big pumping system installed, possibly using natural passages in the rock. Could those passages possibly be an escape route for me? If I could get out to the open sea, that meant we both had a chance to escape. We'd have to deal with the stun-ring on Miranda's leg, and we'd still be monsters. But there would be a *chance* for us to get away from here, together, when it had seemed there was none.

But why would Dr Franklin leave an open door like that? Or as good as open. There must be some catch. He'd made sure Miranda couldn't really escape, before he opened the aviary. Maybe that was because he thought *she* was still human, but that I was a dumb animal, and I wouldn't think of escaping.

I looked at the cover from every angle. I felt it all over with my mouth, and brushed it with the tips of my wings; I gave it a soft, underwater slap with my tail. The hinges were recessed into the turquoise-painted concrete. There was a lip on the other side from the hinges, flush with the wall. It didn't seem to be locked, or fastened in any way. The water pushing against it was enough to keep it closed. If I could get some part of myself under that lip, I could easily heave it open. But I had no hands, no beak, and no teeth in my plankton-filtering mouth.

My tail wasn't any use. I *badly* wanted a pair of hands, or some kind of levering tool. Or a big, strong beak, or gripping tentacles . . . Or else I needed Miranda. If she could get down here, she'd've had it open at once, with her beak or her feet. I'd watched her, over the days we'd spent in this enclosure. A bird is definitely the busy kind of animal. She was always picking things up in one foot and investigating them, or tearing them apart with her beak – flowers, seedcases, sticks, leaves.

Unfortunately, Miranda wasn't built for diving.

So that answered my question. The sluice cover wasn't an open door, if there was no way a fish could open it. I studied it, and felt it with my mouth again. I tried to slip the edge of a wing under the lip, which didn't work. Then I accidentally went off into a dream about tunnels, and pipes, and pumping machinery. Pipes going round corners, water pouring down a deep shaft, the whooshing, splooshing noises that I could hear down there in the dark . . .

The 'hands' thing worried me. I was afraid Miranda had a much better chance of staying human than I did. Unless we escaped soon, I would be the weak link again. I'd go off into one of my long, fish-mind dreams, 'fall by the wayside' and become simply a weird animal, like Dr Franklin said. Then we'd both be trapped forever, because I was sure Miranda would never leave me, even if she got the chance.

I decided I needed to talk to her.

I 'called', flipping the mental switches that should put us in contact.

She wasn't in the enclosure. She spent a lot of time flying free. Sometimes when she was out there, I couldn't reach her on radio telepathy. I'd call her up and get nothing but a blank feeling, sort of like the 'no network coverage' message on the screen of a mobile phone. Either there were parts of the valley that were out of range, or Miranda had somehow switched off the telepathy phone. I tried not to worry when this happened.

I was getting 'no coverage' now.

Miranda! I 'called' again. *Come in, Miranda!*

Suddenly her presence was there, with a feeling like a flurry of wings—

'Yeah, Semi? What is it?'

'Oh, nothing much,' I said, trying to make it casual. 'I want to ask you about something interesting, that's all. When you get back.'

'On my way!'

I was lonely when she wasn't around, but I was very glad for her. I knew she was often desperately bored in the enclosure. (I was never bored. Manta rays don't get bored). I looked forward to her reports too. But it was a real problem, not being able to trust the radio telepathy. I knew she was doing a lot of exploring, but she could never tell me if she'd found out anything that mattered to us.

What mattered to us, of course, was the hope of escape.

Apart from the time he'd come to put the ring on Miranda's leg, Dr Franklin hadn't been back. He'd said nothing about us being the future of the human race, that second time. He hadn't shown any sign of fear either. While the orderlies were opening the roof he'd 'talked' to us the way people talk to their pets. *What a good bird you are Miranda, letting us put the tag on so nicely: very good, well done, here's some extra fruit for you. Hello Semi are you being a good fish, aren't you lucky to have such a nice pool. Aren't you two lucky to have this lovely cage? Are you eating up your plankton Semi?*

Sickening.

We didn't know what to make of this.

Obviously he couldn't talk to us as if we were human when the orderlies were about. He didn't want them to know what he'd done with the two girl castaways. They were supposed to think we were no different from the other animals that had been twisted and changed; new additions to the freak-zoo. But he could have come back alone. Since we'd been put into this enclosure there'd been no IQ testing, no taking of blood samples, no buttons for us to push, no mazes for us to try and solve: nothing. Maybe Dr Skinner and Dr Franklin were watching us on video, but if they were, we hadn't been able to find the cameras. Either they were staying away from us as part of the experiment: or else they really didn't know that we were still human inside.

If Dr Franklin didn't know that we were still human in our minds, if he'd decided that 'the animal traits were too strong', that meant he'd been telling the truth about our radio-telepathy being private. We should have been glad about that. If he wasn't listening when we were talking to each other, that should mean we had a better chance of escaping. But we didn't feel glad. We weren't sensible about Dr Franklin. He had been our god. He had created us. We still felt that crazy kidnap-victim respect for him, the same as we'd felt through the weeks when he'd been torturing us with his 'treatment'. It was mad, but when I thought he'd given up on us, it was as if my dad had rejected me, thrown me out of the house and told me I was no good. I knew it was the same for Miranda, only worse. She'd always been his favourite.

The only thing that made us think the experiment wasn't over was the way both of us could *feel* someone eavesdropping on our radio telepathy conversations.

We were used to assuming that everything we did was watched, everything we said might be heard. This was different. It was *strange*. It was like the feeling you have when someone has walked into the room behind you. You've heard nothing: but you know before you look round that there's somebody there. It was like the feeling you might have on a crowded bus, when you know someone is staring at you. You look around, and some stranger quickly looks away . . . Only stronger than either of those. We had no proof, but we were convinced that someone was 'there'.

We'd managed to tell each other about the eavesdropper without spelling it out in words. We couldn't talk freely on radio telepathy, or in the white place: but our animal selves could communicate. Animals can discuss things, sort of, even if one of them is a ray fish, and the other is a bird. You can do it by closing your eyes or opening them wide. By staring, by the way you move or the way you stand.

Or by the way you swim, in my case.

I didn't like being near the bottom. My fish mind was like a bird's mind in reverse in some ways. I didn't care about the surface of the water being a boundary I couldn't cross: that was natural. I wanted the freedom of the ocean beneath me, not the sky above. If I'd given way to panic, I wouldn't have been trying to leap out onto the dry ground. I'd have been beating myself to death against that hateful turquoise floor.

But I stayed there, rippling my wingtips, thinking, measuring.

I was wondering *how foldable am I?*

I was on the surface when Miranda returned. She came swooping down and landed near me on the pool's rim, with a thump and a bounce that made my water rumble. She spread her glossy wings and preened a little, looking at me significantly.

In my mind, I heard her human voice say, *Semi. Come to the white place.*

I wasn't very keen on the white place. I liked going there

for the notch ceremony, but otherwise I preferred *not* to be reminded of my human body. I didn't want to be thinking about what I'd lost all the time. I wanted to be happy being Semi-the-fish. Besides, all that white stuff made me think of cartoon pictures of angels in heaven, sitting on clouds.

It felt like being dead.

I swam about and splashed the water with my tail, saying: *do we have to?*

Miranda gave a loud caw, and flapped her great wings, saying: *trust me!*

So we flipped those mental switches and we were there, in the white cloud.

Miranda stood with her arms folded. She was looking excited.

'Did you have a good flight?'

'I'll tell you all about it. But what was it you wanted to ask me?'

I noticed that the eavesdropper feeling was very strong. Either it was getting stronger all the time, or I was getting able to notice it more. It was horribly frustrating. I wanted to know what was making Miranda look so excited. I wanted to tell her about the sluice covers and the pumped seawater. The fact that I might have a chance to get out changed everything. I'd have to think of some way to tell her in code. Back in our sham hotel suite we'd learned to disguise what we were talking about, whenever we had anything to say that might be about an escape plan. But I'd always been hopeless at it. I'm a nerd. I do straightforward information. I don't do 'hints'.

'Well, I found out something interesting. Miranda, do you know how far it is to the east coast from here?'

Like Semi-the-fish, Miranda-the-bird was good at judging distances. 'It's what humans call two kilometres fifty, on the ground. The quickest way is by the footpath that leads from the gate in the fence. Where Dr Skinner was going to let us out, you remember. I can see where that path comes out on the east shore, when I'm up high. It's fun going right up high.' She wasn't supposed to soar above the crater rim, but she did it. She'd got away with it so far.

'That's *interesting*! What about the distance to the north coast? And the south?'

'I haven't thought about it.'

'I wish you could find out. It's my new hobby,' I explained, 'Did you know, measurements can be very *interesting*. Like, for instance, how far is my pool above sea level? If you could stretch a piece of string, from my pool to the sea, through the rock, how long would that be? It'd be interesting to know. I like measuring interesting things, you know I do.'

If there was a pipeline running through a tunnel to the sea, I thought the inlet/outlet had to be on the east shore. If there'd been anything like that on our beach, we'd have found it: and we knew, from Miranda's dodgy high-flying trips, that the north and south ends of the island were trees and swamp, right down into the ocean.

'I'd say we're about two hundred and fifty metres above the sea here,' said Miranda. 'The rim of the cone is much higher, of course. I haven't thought about how high, but I will if you like. I don't mind collecting measurements for you. But don't get too interested, Semi. You know that if I fly above the crater rim too often I'll get zapped.'

She pointed to her ankle. I saw a black rubber bracelet around it, like the ring on her bird leg. We saw the stun ring like this, although otherwise we looked like the castaways we used to be. I suppose it appeared in the mental world because it was a sign that we were prisoners, something we thought about a lot. The word 'interesting' was code for anything to do with escape plans. We'd agreed on this ages ago, back in the fake hotel room. Miranda was warning me not to use it too much. She was much better at hinting and talking in riddles than I was.

I could see she hadn't the slightest idea what I was trying to say. I decided to be more direct, and simply tell her about the sluice. I could say it was a nice way to get a massage. I could say it was fun to sit down there where the water came pumping in, *through a big pipe,* straight from the sea—

Miranda had other ideas. 'I'm happy to talk about measurements,' she said, her eyes very bright. 'But I'd like it better if we could play a game. Do you want to play a game that I've thought up? Sort of a *personality* game?'

'Okay.' I wondered what she was up to.

'Good, because I hate being boring. Like poor old *Arnie.* He was so boring, wasn't he?'

That took me by surprise. Neither of us had spoken about our fellow castaway for a long time.

'*Arnie?* What's he got to do with anything?'

We knew, from the evidence we'd found, that Arnie had found the way to the secret valley, nearly a month before we'd stumbled into it. We also knew he'd been caught. I was certain that he'd been treated the same way we had been, but he'd died, instead of being turned into a monster. That was why Dr Franklin had told us we were his 'first human subjects'. Not that he'd have worried about frightening us, but it wouldn't have fitted well into his boasting lecture, the day we arrived – to admit he'd already tried and failed to create a transgenic human.

'I don't know,' said Miranda staring at me hard. 'I don't know what to think. But I know that if we are angry or shocked or upset we turn up here, without meaning to.

That's the way it happened the first time, remember? Visible. Alive and kicking. It might not work, but it's worth trying.'

'What on earth are you talking about?'

'I'm talking about *Arnie*. That prize dork, Arnie Pullman.'

'I don't get it, Miranda.' I was afraid she was going crazy. 'Arnie's dead.'

'Oh, is he? Then let's see if we can raise his ghost. The two of us, summoning him as hard and nasty as we can, that ought to do it. *I think I found out something, Semi.*'

I couldn't believe what she was telling me, but I got the idea, and I went along with it.

'Arnie?' I groaned, 'Do I have to talk about stupid annoying porky dorky *Arnie*?'

Miranda grinned. She knew I'd got the message. 'Yes, that slobby creep *Arnie*.'

We both laughed, as unkindly as we could. In the white place, where emotions were all stripped naked, the effect was hateful. Miranda's face looked like an evil Hallow'een mask. I was almost scared . . . but then I forgot about being scared because something began to happen. The sense that there was someone with us gave a jump in strength. The vague presence took shape. It was familiar. I could *recognise* it—

My mouth dropped open. Miranda nodded fiercely.

'He was most boring of all about *that raft*,' I said. 'He loved it as if it was his baby.'

'Oh yecch, the *raft*!' laughed Miranda, instantly following me. 'That idiotic raft!'

'It was pathetic. You'd have thought he was building a space shuttle—'

'Instead of something that wouldn't have floated across a kiddies' paddling pool.'

'He thought it was so wonderful. It was falling apart, because he couldn't tie knots.'

'All the poles were different lengths—'

'And he hadn't smoothed them off, so it was all lumpy and gappy—'

The cloudy whiteness of the mind-place quivered with outrage. 'Yeah,' said Miranda vindictively. 'The fat creep wasted our twine. And he thought he deserved extra food, because he was "working" so hard . . . Do you remember when he took the bananas?'

I rolled my eyes. 'That was so utterly pathetic and sad. Taking our best food, eating it all himself and then *lying about it!* As if it could have been anybody else!'

'*I did not take the bananas!* The ants took them.'

The voice came from nowhere. We both gasped and grinned.

'Oh sure,' said Miranda. 'Ants. They carried three full-sized wild bananas away. And buried the peel behind the big boulder. You are such a pitiful liar, Arnie.'

A patch of the whiteness blurred, took on colour: and *there he was.*

Arnie!

There was Arnie Pullman, our castaway friend, sitting on the white cloudy 'floor', wearing the salt-stained remains of his black, baggy 'happy face' Nirvana teeshirt and his baggy jeans, exactly the way he'd looked when we last saw him on the beach; his dark hair bristle short, though not quite as shorn as it had been at Miami airport. He stared at us, totally amazed.

We stood there, grinning in triumph.

'What's going on?' he croaked.

'I haven't spent all my time flying up in the sky,' said Miranda to me, ignoring Arnie. 'I've been exploring the compound and watching the orderlies. I hop around pretending to be a dumb-animal bird, and nobody takes any notice. They must have been told to leave me alone. I spotted that the prison-hospital building was being kept locked up, and nobody was getting in there except Skinner or Dr Franklin. I thought about it, and I knew who the prisoner had to be. I put that together with the way we've been *feeling*, Semi, and I decided this might work.'

Arnie was holding up his hands, and staring at them. He peered down at his body, and wailed, 'Where am I? What is this?'

'I don't know,' said Miranda, turning on him fiercely. 'You tell me, you *traitor*. Dr Franklin told us he couldn't eavesdrop on our radio telepathy. We didn't believe him, *but it's true, isn't it*? That's why he's using you. You've got one of those microchips in your brain. You're listening to us, and reporting everything to him. Am I right?'

'Miranda,' I tried to calm her. 'We don't know he's a traitor yet—'

'Am I dreaming?' whispered Arnie. He stretched out his arms, he lifted his legs and looked at his bare feet. He looked as if he might be going to faint – if a mental image can faint. 'Have I been asleep in bed, all this time? What if it's *all been a nightmare*?'

I saw that he looked *different,* the same as Miranda had looked different to me the first time we met here (we didn't notice that effect much, by now). The real Arnie, apparently, was not so nasty and cynical as all that. In the white place, you could see through the annoying *I-know-you-don't-like-me* front, to the lonely, misfit person underneath. His mental image body didn't look chunky and solid. He was still big, but squashy and soft, like a crab without its shell. His mouth was trembling, as if he was going to cry. I said, 'Miranda, you'd better back off. He's going to flip out.'

'*What have you done to me?*' demanded Arnie, in a bewildered moan.

'It's all right Arnie,' I said, 'it's only a stronger signal. Usually, it's voices. But if you kind of mentally shout you end up here, and visible. Like a sort of videophone.'

'Voices in my head,' muttered Arnie, 'Cap full of wires. Brainwaves on a screen.' Then he seemed to pull himself together. He stared around. 'This . . . this is unbelievable. How did you make me appear?'

'We didn't do anything, Arnie,' said Miranda. 'You did it yourself. Like Semi said, you shouted, you turned up the volume. Strong emotions, like anger or fear or a guilty conscience make the radio telepathy into a video link. I don't know how to describe it scientifically, but that's what seems to happen. I mean, you *did* take the bananas, didn't you? Out of pure greed. And obviously you felt guilty about it.'

Arnie tried to put on his old, annoying grin. 'Well, yeah, I took 'em . . . 'Course I did. But I didn't feel guilty. Not me. I didn't really want 'em, I did it to wind you up.'

It didn't work. We could see exactly how ashamed and stupid he felt, about having taken the bananas and then lied about it. We didn't say anything. We didn't have to. He knew. He scowled, and shrugged. 'Okay, okay. All right. You smoked me out. Can we forget the stupid bananas? We're back in contact. Now what?'

Slowly, the three of us sat down, staring at each other.

Miranda said, 'Tell us what's going on.'

Arnie gave a sort of choked laugh. 'Well, you guessed it, Marvellous Miranda. The Doc, Dr Franklin, genuinely can't spy on you. No one can, unless they have the implant.

140

Radio telepathy isn't like ordinary radio. They can't tune in and hear what we're saying, they can only tell when the chips are active. They'd need to have you in the lab, wired up, to listen-in on your conversations directly, and that wouldn't be convenient, the way you are now. He's going to improve the system, but that's the way it works so far.'

'So Miranda's right,' I said. 'You've had the same kind of implant put into your brain. You can pick up our signals as speech the way we can, and you can talk so you can tell him what we're saying. You're his spy.'

Arnie shuddered, '*No*! It isn't like that!'

'Then what is it like?' demanded Miranda.

Arnie's tongue came out, and licked his dry lips. The Arnie we'd known on the beach would have jeered at us and kept on lying, but the white place made lying difficult. Or maybe Arnie had changed, since we'd last met him.

'All right, I give in. Yeah, it's true. That's about it. He's using me. I'm spying.'

We'd told him that we knew what he was doing, but it was a shock to hear him say it. We couldn't speak. We stared at him in horror. Arnie cowered, as if we were hitting him.

'Don't look at me like that,' he pleaded. 'Let me *explain*. Let me tell you—'

It was Day Eighty-Five. We hadn't seen him since Day Eleven, when he'd vanished along with his raft. Back then, Miranda and I had thought he was food for the sharks.

'That's a good idea,' said Miranda coldly. 'We'd like to hear your explanation. You know what happened to us. Your friends Dr Skinner and Dr Franklin have told you everything, I'm sure. So tell us what happened to you. Tell us the whole story, from the day you disappeared. How did you get caught?'

141

'From the day I disappeared? That seems like a long, long time ago. I'll try. Don't blame me if I don't remember all the details.'

'We two went off foraging,' I prompted him, 'Early in the morning. Then what?'

It was like old times, like being on the beach again, the three of us sitting together.

'I was going to work on my raft,' said Arnie. 'But I'd run out of rope, and I wanted to think about redesigning it anyway. I took the twine ball, you know, the remains of the salvaged twine you two had picked up, and went up to the waterfall.'

Miranda and I glanced at each other. Typical! He'd been supposed to stay at the camp.

'I had a swim. Then I started knotting bits of twine together, sitting there in the cool. I got bored of that, so I decided to have another go at climbing the cliff.'

'You found the passage,' said Miranda.

'That's right. I found the passage. I got through into the crater valley. I was in the trees outside the cave, staring down at the buildings. Then there were these goons in uniform, crashing around in the undergrowth. They seemed to be searching for something.'

'Oh!' I exclaimed. 'I bet they were looking for the piglet!'

'What piglet?'

'One of Dr Franklin's animals,' said Miranda. 'It had escaped. It got down into our bay somehow. Semi saw a wild pig mutant when we were in the woods up to the north. But she couldn't believe her eyes. Go on, what next?'

'I suppose that explains it. I thought they were looking for me. I thought I must have triggered some kind of alarm. I'd dropped my machete. That's how I got caught. I was

142

searching round for it, when suddenly the goons were all over me. The weird thing was, they didn't seem *surprised*. They didn't go "who are you and how did you get here", or anything like that. I can speak a bit of Spanish. I tried to talk to them, but they weren't interested. They stuck me in their jeep. The guy who seemed to be the captain of the crew talked to someone on a mobile phone. Then he sent some of his men off up the track. The rest of us waited around for a long time; and no one would talk to me, and they wouldn't let me out of the jeep. In the end the men came back, *with my raft.* I couldn't understand how they'd done that . . . Skinner told me later, there's a place where you can get through the rim of the crater easily, but you can't see the cleft from below, and that's why we never found it. Anyway, they'd been down to the beach, to our camp, and brought it back. I didn't understand what was going on at all, but when they started to break up my raft, I was angry and I sort of, well, started a fight. That's when I was knocked out.'

'Sounds familiar,' said Miranda.

'They had to take the raft,' I pointed out. 'It was too soon to be sure we wouldn't be rescued. It was only ten days after the crash. They didn't want me and Miranda telling anyone about another castaway, who had mysteriously disappeared. With the raft gone, there was no mystery. We had an explanation.'

'Yeah . . . The sharks. I worked that out, later on. But getting back to my story, the next thing I knew I was in a bed, in a prison ward with bars all round me, and nutty Dr Skinner was peering into my cage. That's when . . . it's true, I told him about you two. But I *didn't betray you*! The goons already knew about the camp on the beach, before they picked me up. I was only telling Skinner what he already knew.'

143

'That's what he said to us,' I said. 'They knew were were there all along.'

'Yeah. They were watching us, and we never guessed. They knew about the plane crash the night it happened. I asked Skinner once, what about the other survivors, the ones in the life rafts? Did Dr Franklin know they were there and let them die? Skinner said there weren't any. No one survived the explosion, except us. I suppose that could be true.'

'He told us the same thing,' said Miranda. 'Go on, what happened next?'

'I didn't know anything was wrong. I thought Skinner was a strange character, but everything was going to be okay, and it was only the security staff who had been over-enthusiastic, knocking me out like that. Skinner did some medical tests, gave me some IQ tests, and said they were going to "keep me under observation"; and I *still* thought it was okay. I thought I was going to be sent home, and I couldn't understand why you hadn't been brought in. I realise now they were waiting for some kind of "all clear". Something to make them sure no one would ever come looking for three teenage castaways.'

Miranda and I nodded.

'All three of us are missing-believed-dead.' I agreed, bitterly. 'We don't exist.'

'Yeah,' said Arnie. 'That's what Skinner told me, in the end. That was the main message of the pep-talk, after he'd taken me to see the big Doc. *You're officially dead. We can do what we like, don't try to resist.* But I don't know how long I was kept in the ward, before that happened. My memory is fuzzy. I was ill for a few days. It could be that they drugged me to make me ill, I don't know. Then one fine day he told me I was going to meet the boss. He took

144

me to see Dr Franklin . . . and I finally found out what kind of hellhole place I'd landed in. Yeah, what a hellhole. There've been times, there've been plenty of times in the past weeks, when I've wished the sharks could have had me—'

'So what then?' said Miranda, sternly. 'What happened after the pep-talk?'

'You know what? I escaped, once. They were moving me between the ward and the science block and I was left alone for a few minutes, in a room with an unlocked window. I got out. I hid in the back of a jeep and got driven into the farmland. I thought if I could get away from headquarters, away from Franklin and Skinner, I'd find someone who would help. I hid in the fields until dark, out there where the staff families live, and I went and knocked on a door. A woman let me in. I tried to tell her what had happened, with my bit of Spanish. She gave me some chicken soup . . . shut me in her kids' bedroom, and called the labs. The uniformed branch came and took me away.'

He broke off, and looked at us earnestly. 'I don't blame her. I was a crazy foreign kid, babbling about torture and monsters, and Dr Franklin is the big kind boss who can do no wrong. But remember this. Don't trust them! Don't trust any of them! Everyone on this island is working for Dr Franklin, and if they say they'll help you, they're lying.'

We didn't say anything. I'm sure Miranda was thinking the same as I was.

He was warning us against himself. We couldn't trust Arnie, either.

Arnie resumed his story. 'Then they wasted no more time. A few hours after they got me back I was in the operating theatre, having a microchip stuck into my brain. They kept me out of sight when you two turned up. It was

145

part of the plot, one of Dr Franklin's games, that you weren't to know I was still around, or what had happened to me. When you were out of the way they moved me back to the prison ward. I've been there ever since. When you were, um, ready, they activated my chip. They tuned me in to Radio Mutant and started monitoring your calls . . . And that's about it.'

We looked at him in silence. Something was missing from his story. For a moment (sitting there in my mental-image human body), I couldn't think what it was.

'You had a microchip stuck in your brain,' repeated Miranda. 'That's it?'

'Yeah.'

'You mean *you are still human*?'

'Yes,' he whispered.

Suddenly I could feel the water around me. I could feel the big, slimy delta-shape that was the real Semi now. I stared at Arnie. I tried to imagine what it was like to be him. Was he lying on his bed? Was he sitting on the floor? What was he doing with his hands?

'But you claim you're a prisoner.' said Miranda, softly.

'Of course I am! You don't think I'm sticking around of my own free will?'

'What kind of a person are you, Arnie?'

'My name's Arnie Pullman. I used to live in Surrey, until the lucky day I was in a plane crash. Now I live on a desert island with a mad scientist. When I grow up, I want to be—'

'Cut that out. You know what I'm asking. *How can you work for him?*'

'I have no choice! Do you think I want to spy on you? They keep me locked up. I'm helpless! Look, *I can tell you things.* And I can keep secrets, some of the time. He . . . he doesn't hear every word we say. He doesn't know about this "white place" effect, and I won't tell him. Not if I can help it, I swear—'

'Semi thought you were dead,' said Miranda viciously. 'But you know what? I was never sure. Somehow I knew you'd have squirmed out of trouble. You always managed to sneak out of the dirty jobs.'

'Listen to me, will you. There's something you've got to know. *You mustn't escape.*'

Miranda and I looked at each other—

'Oh yeah?' said Miranda, dangerously calm. 'Why not? Not that we have any plans. We're about as trapped and hopeless as we could possibly be.'

'I'm not asking you to tell me anything. I don't want to know your plans. But you have to stay in the cage. *You haven't had the other half of the treatment.*'

'What are you talking about?' said Miranda, after a stunned silence.

'The antidote. The infusion that turns you back into human beings.'

I don't think there was anything crueller he could have said.

He looked at our faces, our expressions of misery and despair—

'*I'm not lying.* You think I'd lie to you about something like that?'

'You slimy creep,' snarled Miranda. 'You'd lie about anything.'

Arnie bristled. He was getting used to the white place effect, I could tell, and getting back to his normal annoying self. 'Hey, Wonder Girl, get a grip on that temper. What happened to you is not my fault. I'm trying to help. I'm telling you, you have to stay put, for all our sakes—'

'You *snake*!'

Miranda hated snakes more than anything.

She'd jumped to her feet. She looked so *strange,* and the whole white place felt so full of her anger . . . I knew what was going to happen before it happened, but it was still a shock. All the cloudy stuff suddenly started moving, whirling around. Miranda vanished, and then out of that spinning tornado of mental energy came Miranda-the-bird, bigger than in life. She leapt into the air, talons outstretched, her great wings beating—

'You think I'd leave!' she screeched, her red hooked beak savagely wide open, 'You think I'd escape, *when Semi can't get out!* You think I'd leave her behind?'

One of her wings swiped at him. He fell on his back and sprawled, frantically trying to squirm out of reach, yelling in terror, and she plunged down, grabbing at him furiously. As her talons grasped him, I couldn't see the teenage boy any longer. I saw a snake, a writhing limbless thing, as if Miranda had taken control of this whole mental space, and was making him appear in the form she hated. She was shaking him like a rag; and the most terrifying thing was, I could feel *Miranda* slipping away. I could feel her human presence vanishing, so there was nothing left but this nightmarish creature, with the mind of a bird of prey—

I was trying to yell, *stop it, stop it*—

But something was happening to me too. My breath was coming in gasps.

I was choking, my lungs were burning!

I couldn't breathe!

Miranda's rage had overwhelmed me too. I was losing my ability to hold on to this illusion of human form. I was still in the white place, but there was no water and I couldn't breathe! I couldn't breathe!

I blacked out. I fell back into my fish-body. There was water around me, my lungs filled with blessed breathableness. I heard Miranda calling my name.

I flipped the mental switches as hard and fast as I could. I was back with them in the white place, flat on my back, my head spinning. Two worried faces peered down at me.

'Please, Miranda,' I said, sitting up, coughing. '*Don't do that again.* If you have to fight with Arnie, imagine yourself as an all-in wrestler or something.'

'I'm sorry,' said Miranda. She was looking very shaken.

'Next time you two do that, I'll imagine the place full of water, and *drown* you both—'

'I'm really sorry! I couldn't control it. I . . . I boiled over. He provoked me.'

'You did provoke her, Arnie.'

There was a pause, while we all recovered.

'This "white place" is *dangerous*,' I said. 'Place, state of mind, whatever you want to call it. I think we should stay out of it. I think we're better off as monsters.'

The other two looked as if they agreed with me. Then Miranda said, in a quiet voice, 'Tell us about the antidote, Arnie. Not that we believe you.'

'The whole idea was to turn us into mutants,' I added. 'To see if he could do it, if he could make us into superhumans. Why would he want to turn us back?'

Arnie looked at us as if we were idiots. 'You're kidding. Of course he wants the process to be reversible! Eventually, when it works. Nobody would want to be half-fish or half-bird for life, would they?'

I don't think he realised how cruel he was being. I truly hated Arnie, at that moment.

Miranda took it differently. She said, her eyes bright, 'You mean . . . there *is* a purpose in what happened to us?

149

It's not just crazy and cruel? How much do you know, Arnie? He talked about interplanetary travel. He said that was his goal. Is that actually the truth?'

I looked at the ground, feeling very sad. Poor Miranda. She was trying to keep the hope out of her voice, but it was there. After everything he'd done to her, Miranda still wanted to believe in Dr Franklin's dreams. I understood why, but I thought she was totally deluded.

Arnie shook his head. 'Nah, nothing like that. Don't be daft. Interplanetary travel? That's science fiction. I reckon if they manage to iron out the problems, they'll be selling their formula to an exotic holiday company.'

'Holiday company?' I repeated, confused. 'What on earth do you mean?'

'They talk in front of me, you see. I've heard a lot of things. He's hoping to reduce the timescale of the first change, which is the remaining big hitch. When he's got that down to a few hours, he'll have a commercial proposition. Imagine it. You take a pill, or a couple of injections. Like being vaccinated. They put you in a flotation tank overnight, while the ugly stuff is going on. You wake up in a five-star underwater hotel, on your ocean safari. Or in some kind of luxury cliffside flying lodge, on the wall of the Grand Canyon. Spend two weeks exploring the deep ocean, or flying like a bird, then go through the same thing in reverse. The way it works now is no good. What happened to you two is a bust, no one would buy it. But I can see people paying for the improved version of the change, in the future. Can't you?'

'I hate you, Arnie,' said Miranda. 'You are lower than dirt.'

I thought of our days and weeks of pain and terror, of all the hideous things that had been done to us. I thought of the morning when I'd seen Miranda's breastbone bursting through the flesh and skin. And this would be reduced to a few hours' sleep, a holiday in a brochure.

I thought of us, Miranda and me, as discards, spoiled attempts to be thrown in the bin.

'Sorry,' said Arnie, grinning defiantly. 'I didn't mean to give offence. Look, forget the dumb Startrek daydream. Face up to reality. I want to do a deal. If I get you the antidote, will you take me with you?'

That was so like Arnie. If he was begging for his life, he would have to be annoying about it. Miranda and I looked at each other. It was ironic, Arnie asking us for help. He was still human. We were the ones in serious, horrible trouble.

Miranda said, 'Are you going to go on spying for him? Reporting on us?'

Arnie licked his lips, and shuddered. 'Yes.'

'Then you can rescue yourself!'

'Miranda, *I have to*. You don't know how it works. I'd have told you what was happening from the start, only *I couldn't*. I didn't know how.'

'Liar. You're working for Dr Franklin. You don't want us to escape because then you'd be next in line for the treatment. You're afraid that if you don't do what he says, he'll turn you into a monster anyway. A monster like us.'

'Yeah!' shouted Arnie. '*I'm afraid*. Not everyone can be as brave as you, Wonder Girl. I'm afraid that if I don't co-operate, not that I have any choice, something worse will happen. Look, I'll tell him as little as I can. He won't find out that we've made contact, if I can help it. Don't try to escape, and I'll try to get the antidote to you.'

'I told you,' said Miranda. 'There is no escape plan.'

'But *I know there is*. I know you never give up. *Please*

say you'll take me with you. When you're human again, you'll come to the ward and you'll get me out? *Please*?'

Miranda stood up, and started pacing around. She kept looking at Arnie, and he kept looking at her. It was the same as on the beach. I didn't think Miranda was totally in the right, but I didn't want to side with Arnie, so I stayed quiet. At last she came back, and stood there, arms folded and her head on one side, looking very birdlike.

'You're Dr Franklin's stooge. You're a treacherous snake, and you've been allowed to stay human so you'll spy on us and help him play his mind-games. How can we possibly trust you? But if *by any chance* there is such a thing as this antidote—'

Then she did something horrible. She lifted one leg, and stretched it out. The rest of her stayed the same as Miranda the castaway, a sunburned skeleton with long black raggedy hair, in her old grey combat shorts and black teeshirt. But the leg became her bird's leg: thin and scaled and leathery. She wasn't out of control this time. She was doing it on purpose, she was showing Arnie who was in charge. The leg stretched out, impossibly long and muscular. The bird's foot, with its long, strong scaly fingers and fearsome talons, took hold of him by the front of his teeshirt and hauled him to his feet.

'You bring it to us. You get that stuff to us, some way. Or I will kill you. I don't know how I'll do it, but I swear I will kill you.'

10

For a couple of days after that, nothing happened. We stayed in our animal bodies. We didn't talk to each other on radio telepathy much. I swam up and down the pool, being my fish-self, thinking long thoughts. Miranda flew about the crater valley. Sometimes I'd see her overhead, or hopping on the ground outside our enclosure. Sometimes I'd hear her shrieking, somewhere else in the compound. I'd know she'd been getting too near one of the orderlies, and they'd chased her away. We only called each other up last thing at night, to cut our imaginary notch on the imaginary coconut palm. We didn't care if we were overheard doing that.

It's strange how things turn out the opposite of what you'd expect. You'd have thought 'the white place' would have been a wonderful discovery, a place where we could go (if only in our minds) where we could remember what being human was like. But it made everything worse, not better.

You'd have thought finding out that the experiment was still going on would have cheered us up. It was nasty to know that Arnie was Dr Franklin's spy, but at least we hadn't been abandoned like pieces of rubbish. But it didn't work like that. Sometimes it's better to have no hope. You can find a way to live with what you have left. Before we caught Arnie, we'd been almost *happy*, as Semi-the-fish and Miranda-the-bird. Maybe we were going to live our lives as weird animals in Dr Franklin's zoo, but we weren't in pain, we had our radio-telepathy, and at least we were near each other. Now Arnie had told us we could be human again, and we didn't believe him but it was terrible. It was like someone hitting you on a bruise. It was like someone making you try to walk with a broken leg.

On Day Eighty-Seven, a small plastic tube appeared on the tiled rim of my pool.

I spotted it first, and called to Miranda – not by telepathy but by slapping my tail on the water.

Neither of us knew how it had got there. Our animal selves were daytime creatures. We'd found out that we couldn't stay awake at night, no matter how hard we tried. Miranda would roost in the mango tree, at the end of the pool furthest from the gate, where the shelter of the trees and bushes was thickest. I would let myself sink a little, into the lower water, and drift there. Someone must have sneaked into the enclosure under cover of darkness, and left us this little mystery. But who? Arnie had told us he was a prisoner. The tube was about the length of my little finger (the finger I had when I was a girl, I mean), and about a finger wide. It was clear plastic with a white screw top, and half filled with a greenish white powder. Miranda picked it up in her foot. In my mind, her voice said softly, 'Semi. What do you think?'

This was too complicated for sign-language. We had to risk being overheard.

'If it's the antidote,' I said, (thinking about the antidote had been a big part of my long fish-thoughts, since we'd talked to Arnie), 'then I expect it's some form of our original DNA. You can dry out DNA. I know there's such a thing as powdered DNA, and DNA pellets. If we were dosed with a strong infusion of our original girl genetic information, I suppose it could take over again and crowd out the altered DNA. I don't know. Something like that might work.'

Miranda-the-bird looked at me hard.

'So this would be powdered Semirah? Or powdered Miranda? Or both?'

'It might be.'

'The tube is cold, very cold.'

'They probably keep it in a fridge. It can't have been here long.'

'How are we supposed to know what to do with it?'

'We'd better ask Arnie,' I said.

We were both silent for a minute. We were listening (that's the best way to describe it) for the eavesdropper on our telepathic link. If he was there, he was keeping very quiet. So we called him, both of us calling his name in our minds.

It took a couple of tries before he answered.

'Okay,' said Arnie's voice in my 'head' – inside my delta-shape *me*, but humans say 'head' – 'The stuff is for Semi. It won't do anything for Miranda, so don't try sharing it. I haven't managed to get hold of Miranda's antidote yet. It'll be more difficult. It doesn't matter, because Semi's will take longer to work. You have to sprinkle this powder into the pool, and she has to swallow it. It'll take several doses. You'll find the tubes on the side of the pool, the same way as this one.'

'How did the tube get in here, Arnie?' said Miranda's voice on the chatline, coldly. 'And what's this about stealing from the labs? You told us you were a prisoner.'

'There's a friendly lab technician. I don't completely

155

trust him, but he feels sorry for us and he'll do things. When Semi's had enough of the antidote, there's a plan to get her out of the pool and away to safety. That's all I can say.'

'Why didn't you tell him to get Miranda's antidote?' I asked.

Silence . . . Then Arnie's voice said, 'I told you, getting hold of Miranda's stuff is going to be more difficult. I'm working on a plan.' He sounded very uneasy and shifty. 'I can't talk any more. Remember, they've got me wired up. Whatever I tell them, they can see what's been happening by looking at the brain-wave print out. They'll spot that I've been talking as well as listening, if we don't keep it snappy. Then they'll know I'm double-crossing them. I have to shut up now.'

The best thing about nailing Arnie was knowing that he was still alive. I could understand how Miranda felt, but even so, that was good news. We three had crawled onto the beach together, on the night of the plane crash. We'd been through the first shock of the castaway experience together. It made me feel more human, to know that he'd survived. The worst thing was that it left us exactly where we'd been before. We couldn't get rid of him: and we couldn't trust him. We still had nowhere to hide.

'Maybe it really is more difficult to get hold of your cure,' I said.

'Or maybe he's getting his revenge, because I scared the living daylights out of him.' She half opened her wings, a kind of bird-monster shrug of the shoulders. 'It doesn't matter. If you can be human again, that would be a miracle enough. We can think about what happens to me later. If *you* can get out . . . well, a bird can always fly.'

She hopped closer to the water.

'What shall I do? This could be dangerous. I don't see any way we can spread it on a small part of you, and see what happens. Do you want time to think about it?'

We both understood that we had no way of knowing what was in that tube. Arnie could be lying, on instructions from the boss. This could be another of Dr Franklin's mind-games. Or Arnie and his friendly technician could have got hold of the wrong chemicals. Or anything. The stuff in the tube could kill me, or plunge me into worse tortures than ever.

'There's nothing to think about,' I said, quickly, so I wouldn't lose my nerve. 'Do it!'

Miranda held the tube in her foot, and twisted at the cap with her strong beak.

My heart was in my mouth, my whole body was shivering with fear and anticipation. The cap came off, and went spinning away. Miranda hopped right up to the rim, and shook the powder into the water.

It fell into the sunlit blue, in little swirls and sparkles.

I dropped under it, and all the swirls and sparkles flowed into my mouth. The water flowed out again through my gills, the powder stayed behind. I knew I had swallowed it, like a mouthful of plankton.

Nothing happened. I felt nothing.

I hovered there, staring up at Miranda, until we heard the rumble of wheels. An orderly was arriving with our food. I glided away, and Miranda flapped up into a tree.

When the man had left again, Miranda was nowhere to be seen. I thought she'd gone for a flight. Then I spotted her, hunched in some tall bamboo grass near the fence, half way down the pool. I swam over and tried to catch her attention. I even leapt out of the water, which is something I can do if I feel like it, but I don't because it's too spectacular, and it makes me feel a bit crazy. (It's my *crush that fishing boat* trick.) She didn't take any notice. Then I remembered. It may sound strange, but I'd forgotten, for a moment, that I had the power of human speech. I flipped those mental switches, and called her up on Radio Mutant.

'Hey, Miranda!'

No coverage.

'Miranda?' I repeated.

She didn't seem to know I was there.

I swam away, feeling very worried.

She was all right later. But it was a warning.

Dr Franklin had said, 'the animal traits are very strong'. How long would we be able to take the strain of trying to stay human, under these impossible conditions? How long before we lost our minds?

Day Ninety.

Something strange happened today. Skinner came to see us.

Things had been quiet. I'd been swimming around, trying to imagine that I felt some change in myself. Miranda had been playing her usual restless games with sticks and leaves, and chasing a few butterflies. We hadn't been using our radio telepathy at all, except for the notch-cutting ceremony: partly because we knew Arnie would be listening, and partly because the uncertainty was too painful to discuss. Either I was going to become human again . . . or I wasn't.

Miranda was out flying when Skinner turned up. He was looking rather shabby. His white coat had grubby stains on the collar and cuffs, and a pen had leaked in the breast pocket. He needed a shave too. He came sidling up to the fence, peering around as if he was afraid one of the orderlies would spot him and chase him away. I came up and looked

158

at him. We shifted along, him on one side of the mesh and me on the other, until we were beside the gate; where there weren't any flowers or bushes between the fence and the rim of the pool, and we had a good view of each other.

'Hello Semi,' he said. 'Where's Miranda?'

Imagine a teenager-sized manta ray shrugging vaguely.

I didn't care if he understood me or not.

'I'm not supposed to be here,' he told me, glancing to and fro again. 'It's bad for the experiment. But I'm a bad boy. I've not been myself since I tried to let you two go.' He laughed miserably. 'Next thing you know, I'll be letting that jungle cat loose . . . can you hear it howl from here?'

Yes we could, sometimes, especially at night. It wasn't a very comforting lullaby.

'How have you been getting on, in your new home?'

I glided up and down, and smacked my tail on the water. Skinner took hold of the fence in both his hands, and leaned his face between them, so the mesh was pressing into his cheeks and up against his glasses.

'It's different close up,' he whispered. 'I thought I knew what seeing you changed was like, but this is bad, this is real . . . I *remember* you, Semi. I remember what you looked like. I think I remember seeing you smile, once—'

I believe Semi-the-fish has the same eyes as Semi-the-girl, at least Miranda says so: although they work much better, if differently. So imagine a teenager-sized manta-ray, with dark blue sheeny skin (where the human girl's skin used to be naturally brown); and brown human eyes looking out of the front of the ray's smooth winged shape. A girl squashed flat, her legs and arms fused to her body and then *rolled out,* like plasticine, into the delta-shape of a big ray fish. That's what Skinner saw. I was used to the idea of the girl-fish. But no wonder he was staring at me with sickened horror.

I wished he'd go away, but I wanted him to stay. I liked seeing him suffer, to tell you the absolute truth. There was no chance that Dr Franklin was going to have any painful pangs of guilt, but Skinner was better than nothing.

'*Are* you there inside the fish, Semi? Do you remember being human? We can't be sure. Human-like brain activity doesn't prove that you can really think and feel, like a human girl. Oh god, I hope you don't! It would be too cruel.'

I didn't know what to do. According to Arnie's story, Skinner should know perfectly well that I had a human mind. He'd been getting reports of Miranda and me chatting to each other. But his gibbering remorse looked genuine, and I couldn't resist feeding it. I zoomed myself backwards from the side, zoomed back up to the rim: stopped myself half a centimetre before I rammed the tiles, and smacked my tail down hard.

Dr Skinner looked like someone who has seen a ghost.

'She's definitely trying to communicate,' he muttered. 'But what kind of mind is in there? That's what we can't know. How changed, how alien? The brain activity might not mean anything. Remember, she may be intelligent, she may be *very* intelligent, but she isn't human anymore.'

Thanks a lot, I thought.

He gave another furtive glance around. There were no orderlies in sight. He darted to the gate, and tapped the keys on the lockpad rapidly (I tried to see, but I couldn't). He slipped inside and came and knelt at the edge of the pool. I was right on the surface. He could have tried to touch me, but he didn't. Shame. I have a sting in my tail. I didn't know if it was seriously poisonous, but I wouldn't have minded trying a little experiment.

'Why don't you swim away, Semi? Aren't you afraid of humans? You should be!'

I stayed where I was, staring up at him as meanly as I could. Manta rays are not very mean by nature, but I did my best to look nasty and accusing.

'Oh God,' muttered Dr Skinner. 'This can't be happening. I'm a scientist. I'm not a—'

Criminal? I wondered. Murderer? Because we had been murdered, Miranda and I. We were worse than dead, if you weren't trying desperately hard to take a positive view—

He swallowed, and wiped his hands on his coat. I saw his Adam's apple jerk up and down. 'Okay,' he muttered. 'I'm a scientist. I'm not supposed to do this, but let me see.' He picked up a handful of pebbles from the gravel border beside the pool. 'Semi, watch me.' He set the pebbles down, in nine little groups, in a row along the tiles. 'The brain activity that we've recorded says you have human minds. Can you show me if that's true? *He* says we mustn't interfere. He says you have to be left alone, the way transgenics might be alone on an alien planet. He's crazy . . . Give me some proof. If you can understand what I'm saying, do what I tell you. Use your mouth, or your tail, or whatever you like, Semi. But you are to move every third bunch of pebbles. You understand? Every third bunch!'

This test, I thought, is unfair on animals with no hands. Not only can I hardly do it, but I don't understand *wanting* to do it. But I'll move the pebbles. To see you squirm.

I got right to the edge, and moved the pebbles into the water, using the soft paddles by my mouth, which are there to guide the plankton the way it should go. Every third bunch. Any manta ray able to swim and chew plankton at the same time could have done it, if they could understand English, (and see the point). I didn't have to have ever been

161

a girl. I didn't much want those dirty pebbles in my water, either, but it was necessary for the cause of scientific progress. Ha.

Dr Skinner's face went chalky white under the red sunburn, right up to his hair. I thought for a horrible moment he was going to fall into my pool. Yeech. But he didn't. He stood up. I could see that he was shaking. He started pacing up and down (he reminded me of Miranda when he did that). Then he came back, got on his knees again, and leaned over the water. 'Suppose I could help you?' he whispered. 'Suppose you could never be truly human again, would you still want to be free?'

I dived. I had a hard time fetching the pebbles up, because my mouth is not built for that sort of thing, but I got a bunch of them up to the rim, and spat them out carefully, in the form of a tick. Like, *yes.* I didn't see any harm in telling him that, it couldn't be a big secret. I hoped it made him feel even more terrible. Of course I wanted to be free.

Dr Skinner stared at this message. His eyes rolled behind his glasses. He turned and scuttled for the gate, locked it and hurried out of my sight.

I wondered if that was the last I'd see of him.

Skinner's behaviour was very puzzling. Why had he suddenly turned up? It must have something to do with the fact that we'd contacted Arnie. But he didn't seem to know that we'd been talking to Arnie . . . What did that mean? I badly, badly needed to talk to Miranda. But talking to Miranda was getting difficult.

Day Ninety-Five (I think).
I have had a second dose. It turned up on the side of the pool, under the mango tree, as before. We've never been

162

sure whether we're under video surveillance in here or not, but I think if there are spy cameras, the tube might be difficult for them to pick up. It's very small, and almost invisible against the tiles. Miranda opened it for me and chucked the powder in the water, and I swallowed it. Still no sign of any antidote for Miranda. At the notch-cutting ceremony that night she said to me, *We don't even know if that's Arnie we've been talking to. It could be Skinner and Franklin, feeding radio signals into our brains, making us see Arnie the way we remembered him, making us hear the voice we remember. We don't know anything, Semi. We can't trust anyone, not even ourselves, not even our own minds. He's taken it all away.*

I'd seen Miranda break down, I'd seen her crying from fear and loneliness. But in all our trials, I'd never, never heard her talk like that before.

She won't say so, but I know it's very hard on her that I have the antidote and she doesn't. I said, I don't want to get back into human form. If you're going to stay a bird, I want to stay a fish. She said *don't be stupid,* and cheered up a bit.

She won't say so, but I know (and she knows I know) that the reason she got so angry with Arnie in the white place, is that *of course* she's thought of flying away and leaving me. If she ever got the chance. She's thought about it. She wouldn't be human if she hadn't thought about it. But she'd never do it.

I haven't told her about Skinner.

I don't know whether I'm right or wrong, but I've decided to keep quiet.

Miranda's right. We don't know who's listening on Radio Mutant. We don't know who to trust. We don't know anything.

We haven't found out how the tubes get here. We've

tried staying awake. We can't do it, not even if we can hear the jungle cat howling. It's good to have a few hours of escape, but it's terrible to feel that our bodies are animal bodies, doing animal things that we can't control. I keep thinking about how horrible it is to be a monster, more and more. I try to drift and have sunlit dreams, but I seem to have lost the knack. It's frightening. If I lose my calm, Semi-the-fish state of mind, I think I'll go crazy.

Maybe I should be worrying about me, not Miranda.

But exciting things have happened! I found a stick floating in the water (the orderly skims the debris out of my pool every day, but this one he'd missed). I started messing with it – copying the things Miranda does, really – and found I could hold it between those mouth-flippers of mine. I would never have thought I could do that. I took it down to the sluice cover, and I poked and pried (dropping my stick a hundred and seven times before I got anywhere). Finally I managed to lever the flap open.

There's a channel full of water. It's tight at first, but it gets wider. That's how much I know so far. I can fold myself enough to squeeze inside, which is brilliant news. I almost feel I'm girl-shaped again when I fold my wings like that. I haven't explored any further. I'm scared that one of the orderlies will come along and notice . . . whoops, there's no mutant manta ray in the water. This pool is worse than our beach. There's *nowhere* to hide. (The story of our life!) But the real problem is that I can't tell Miranda – for the same reason as I can't risk telling her about Skinner. We can't use the radio telepathy for secrets, and I can't think of a way a mutant manta ray can say *I can get out of my pool through a pipe*, by swimming up and down or slapping her tail.

Maybe Miranda has the same problem. The other day, I

was watching her the way I do, because I like watching her. She noticed me, and started bringing things to the rim of my pool. I'd seen her arrange patterns of twigs and flowers before (Miranda says she does it out of boredom, but I think it's very clever and pretty). I came up to admire. I looked and I saw (maybe it was Skinner's pebbles that had put me in the right frame of mind) that she had arranged a pattern of numbers. Five seedpods. Six red flower petals. Three manky pieces of melon rind, nine sticks, two dead butterflies.

I splashed my tail to mean 'that's really nice!' She stared at me furiously, gave a shriek, and swept it all away with her wing.

Afterwards I realised why she was angry with me, and I *think* I know what she meant, but she had gone, flying free again, so I couldn't tell her.

Day Ninety-Eight.
It's very frightening to think how long we've been in this cage. I'm calling this Day Ninety-Eight, but when I try to line up all the days in my memory, I know there are gaps in the record, even since we started the count again. I've taken three doses of the powder now. My body doesn't seem to be changing at all.

We haven't heard from Arnie again. We hardly use the radio telepathy.

We don't want to and . . . I think we both sometimes forget how.

I think we might be turning into dumb animals.

I'm afraid for Miranda. She's hardly here. She spends her whole time flying free: and when she *is* here, she pays less and less attention to me.

Before we were changed Miranda was the strong one,

and I was the one who panicked. Since we were changed, it seems to have been the other way round. Miranda says I've always been the tough one, inside. I don't think that's strictly true. I think it's partly because I have a fish mind and she has a bird mind; and partly just that different people can be brave in different situations. While we were on the beach, and while we were having our 'treatment', it was Miranda's kind of strength we needed. Miranda is a high-flier, always striving to be the best, to get things right. As long as she has something to achieve, she's all right. I'm more of a deep-swimmer, keener on things than people, content with my own thoughts: and that means I'm better able to cope with being locked up and abandoned in a freak zoo. That's the way it seems to me, anyway. We're both strong, we're both weak, in our different ways. But the awful thing is that she helped me, she saved my life a thousand times, and now I don't know how to help her.

When I call her up she doesn't answer. I hear her voice in my mind repeating words and scraps of sentences that don't make sense . . .

Flight . . . aerofoil . . . lift . . . the muscles of the sternum . . . always wanted to be able to fly . . . oh, Semi, always wanted to fly . . .

. . . she's standing right beside my pool, but she sounds as if she's very far away.

I remember thinking that being together as animals was the same as being castaways. We knew each other so well we didn't need to be able to talk, to be company for each other. I was wrong. We're together but there are bars between us, and that's no good. I can't get excited about lifting that sluice cover. I can't bear to think about escaping. It doesn't matter whether we can get out of this enclosure or not. If she doesn't recover her human form soon, *it will be too late.*

On the hundredth day from Miami Airport, as far as I could judge, I woke up in the morning and knew that we had missed the notch-cutting ceremony. I tried to remember if we'd done it the night before, but I couldn't. I couldn't remember if we'd done it the night before that, either.

I swam around, feeling very miserable. I'd been dreaming about being at home with my mum and dad, and it had been dreadful to wake up. I wanted to cry, but my fish-monster eyes couldn't cry. I forgot to use my fins like wings, I tried to lift my arms above the surface – which gave me a horrible straitjacket feeling, as if my arms were swaddled up in a slimy wet sheet, and I couldn't get them free. That panicked me for a few minutes, but I managed to calm myself; only I was very worried about Miranda.

Then I saw her. She was under the mango tree. I knew she was feeling bad, by the droop of her wings. I swam down there. Under the shade of the mango tree was the nearest we could get to being out of sight of the orderlies, or anyone else who might be watching us. I swam up to the rim, and saw the new plastic tube lying there. Another dose. Miranda didn't seem to have noticed it.

I flipped those mental switches, and called to her, 'Hey, Miranda!'

No coverage.

She was standing right in front of me, wide awake, holding a piece of fruit in one foot while she pecked at it with her beak. The bird-monster's head turned sideways, and a bright, empty eye looked at me without any interest.

167

She was *gone*. There was nothing human in that look at all

I was alone, totally alone. Miranda had left me behind, she'd gone ahead of me, on the last stage of our terrible adventure. I seemed to hear, though I knew it was my imagination, the whisper of her human voice, fading away forever:

Exciting, Semi. Say it!

Exciting . . . a great adventure . . .

I knocked the tube into the pool with one of my wingtips.

I didn't have a chance of removing a screw cap. I kept smacking the thing against the side, with my body, until it crumpled. I gobbled the powder as it spilled out, trying to hoover up every single particle. Then there was nothing more for me to do but swim around, praying that something would happen. Praying that the pain and torture of the change would begin.

11

Day One Hundred-and-Two
On Day One-Hundred, Miranda flew away. I didn't
see her leave. She didn't come back by nightfall. I was
awake half the night, afraid she must be lying hurt somewhere. I thought she must have tried to fly beyond the
crater rim, and been zapped out of the sky. In the morning
Dr Skinner and Dr Franklin turned up with some orderlies. They obviously knew that Miranda had gone. They
searched the enclosure. I glided up and down my pool,
wondering what they were looking for. They didn't take
any notice of me. Dr Skinner looked very flustered. The
orderlies shouted at each other in Spanish. Even the animals
in the zoo seemed to be upset. I could hear them hooting
and grunting; and the cat was howling. I thought it was like
the sound of the prisoners in a jail, when they know there's
been a break out.

Dr Franklin looked older. His thick grey hair was
untidy, his face seemed to have more lines. Even the cold
brightness of his eyes seemed dimmed. He stood by my
pool talking to Skinner. I listened carefully. I found out that
we *had* been under video surveillance, but the camera's eye
view didn't show them everything that went on in here.
They'd come along today to search for signs of genuinely
human-like activity that the cameras hadn't picked up, but

they'd found none. They talked about Miranda's flower and twig patterns. They said it proved nothing. Some kinds of real, natural birds (like bower birds) do that sort of thing, and it doesn't mean they're intelligent the way human beings are intelligent. They were saying that the brain-wave readings had fooled them. They thought Miranda had come through the change all right, but she had started to deteriorate soon after, and now she was completely 'non-human'.

Apparently she wasn't lost. They knew where she was. She was out beyond the farmland, in the scrubby forest that covered the rest of the valley floor. They could pick her up any time they liked, but Dr Franklin wanted to observe her for a while. He wanted to see what kind of behaviour she came up with, as a formerly human transgenic bird monster. I heard him say, 'Remember, this is not a human mind! The stun-ring will prevent her from leaving the valley, and from attacking any of the staff. We'll let her settle down, and then go out and study her, get some video record . . . Later, we can bring her in for the vivisection, and find out what's been going on inside. I don't look on this as a failure, Skinner. Not at all! This is exactly what I planned for my prototypes. It has been a very exciting first trial.'

So now I knew why we hadn't been abandoned. Our creator had been watching over us, all right. Watching to see us fall apart in the cause of science. This did not make me feel any better. That strange word *vivisection* frightened me. At first I didn't know why. Then I remembered that it means scientists operating on animals while they're alive, and I was even more frightened.

She's been away two days. I'm very lonely and I'm very scared. I think something's happening to my fish-self. I can feel my human arms and legs again, like phantom limbs inside me. I'm becoming human again, and Miranda is a dumb animal. She doesn't know they know where she is. She doesn't know they'll come after her and bring her back, and cut her open while she's still alive. There's no way I can warn her. I flip the mental switches and call and call, but she doesn't answer me, and Arnie (if that was ever really Arnie) doesn't answer me either. I don't know what to do.

Day One Hundred-and-Three.
Skinner came to the enclosure alone, early in the morning. The shadows were lying long and cool on the water, and some bird like a swallow was darting to and fro, dipping down to the surface to drink and skimming away again. The orderly hadn't come to clean the pool yet. There were a couple of twigs floating on the water; and a bee that had fallen in and drowned. I saw Skinner by the gate, mopping his sun-reddened face with a handkerchief. I hid in the shade of the mango tree.

He opened the door and sneaked inside. Then he came to the edge of the water and knelt down, and lowered something into it. I swam over. I wanted to find out what he was doing. The dangling thing was a kind of big syringe, attached to a box that he held in his hand, with keys to press and a little screen. He didn't look at me, but he knew I was there. 'I'm sampling your water,' he murmured, quietly. 'Now that Miranda's gone, Dr Franklin's decided it's no longer important that we stay away from the enclosure. He wants to know if you are giving off high levels of stress-related chemicals. He wants to know how the disappearance of your companion has affected you.'

Why doesn't he try asking Arnie? I thought. Skinner's glasses were milky with reflected light, the way they'd been that night when he tried to help us to escape. Mad milky-penny eyes. 'I'll have to make sure something happens to this water sample, won't I? I'd better drop it in the lab, or spill a cup of coffee into it. I'm sure you're stressed, but there are other chemicals in this water that shouldn't be here. Aren't there, Semi?'

He bent his head, pretending to look at something on the control box. I suppose the camera eyes that we had never found were still recording.

'We don't want Dr Franklin to know that you are changing back. Do we?'

So Skinner was the 'friendly technician', that Arnie had told us about. That made sense. Who else but Skinner (or Dr Franklin) would have access to the antidote infusion?

All I could do was stare at him.

He looked at the little screen on his box, tapped some keys, and nodded to himself. Then he leaned down closer to me. 'Semi,' he whispered, 'it's time. We have to get you out of here, before it's obvious what's happening to you. There's a way out of the pool. Have you found it? Splash your tail. Once for yes, twice for no.'

I lay there on the surface, rippling my wings, trying to desperately think what I should do now. Should I trust him? How could I trust him?

I splashed my tail.

'Okay,' whispered Skinner. 'We're going to get you out. Listen. Miranda's been seen soaring above the crater. I'm going to take the motor launch tonight and patrol around the island, ready to get a fix on her exact location, if she gets herself zapped and falls on to the mountainside, on the wrong side of the rim. That's my excuse for getting away . . . I'll be at the east coast jetty, at dawn. Your friend Arnie will be with me. You have to get out of the pool, get

172

to the jetty and wait for me there. I hope you can do that. I'm afraid you're on your own, I can't help you. Leave after dark. The cameras in here can't pick up much after night-fall. This is the best I can do, Semi. Don't worry about Miranda. We'll raise a rescue party, and come back for her. Remember, *you have to come to the jetty.* Don't take off for the open sea. The change should be easier this time, but I don't know what it will be like. You may need special care. This is something that's never been tried before. I'll be there, with Arnie. We won't leave without you.'

He fumbled with his water-sampling gadget. Something slipped from his cupped palm into my pool, making a tiny splash. It was another of those little tubes.

'That's your last dose. Take it immediately, then wait for nightfall.' He stood up, wiping his hands furiously on that handkerchief, as if he was trying to wipe away his guilt. 'Miranda was right,' he muttered. 'I should have left with the two of you, that first night. Now it's almost too late. No more games, Semi. This is real. I can't stand to be here, to see what he's going to do to Miranda—'

I was doing absolutely nothing. I was an inquisitive ray fish, floating on the surface, watching this human with his funny machine and his funny mumbling. I kept on doing nothing, showing not a sign of 'human-like activity' until he left.

I let the tube float, while I tried to think. I had no rational reason to trust Skinner. The last time he'd tried to save us he'd let us down badly. I could feel that the doses of powder were doing something to me. If he'd really been giving me the antidote, did that mean the rest of his story was true? But how I could bear to leave without Miranda? What if she came back, and I was gone? I thought about that motor launch, and the tracking equipment. I thought about Arnie-the-eavesdropper. I thought I should call him up, but when I tried he didn't answer, and I realised I didn't dare to trust 'Arnie' anyway. I swam around and around, feeling so alone, trying to figure out a cunning plan that would . . . save me, save Miranda, save Arnie (if he was really still alive!).

In the end I just crushed the tube, swallowed the powder and waited.

The orderly came and skimmed the pool, and fed me my plankton.

I decided I didn't dare trust the radio telepathy at all anymore. Then I decided I had to try, and I called and called for Miranda: but she didn't answer. Not a word, not a sign.

In the afternoon I started to feel ill. I felt hot inside, and shivery outside. If I'd been human, I'd have said I was running a fever. I remembered what my great-grandmother in Jamaica used to say: get out in de good sun, let de heat drive out de fever. But the sun didn't warm me. My thoughts weren't dreamy and slow. They were tangled up and frightening and confused. I tried to remember how happy I had been, cruising around in the water, full of strength and grace, eating plankton as easily as breathing. It was gone. It was as if my mind was a train that had been switched onto a different track. Semi-the-fish was heading off into the distance, and this other Semi was racing back, faster and faster – the girl who had been put through too many horrors, and couldn't take much more.

I kept thinking of what Skinner had said about me needing special care. What if I was further on than he realised? I had not seen myself in my bad time. I only knew how it had been for Miranda. I saw her in my mind: Miranda twisted up in agony, her face fallen in, her breastbone bursting out of her chest. Things like that were going to happen to me. Again, soon. If I stayed in my pool, Dr Franklin would look after me. He'd be angry with me, like a father with a disobedient child. But he would look after me.

I hid in the shade of the mango tree, and watched the swallows dipping over the water. The sun moved across the sky. My head was aching and the inside of my mouth felt strange and sore. How could 'my head' be aching? My head wasn't a separate thing, stuck on, on a little stalk. It was inside me, part of *me*. I felt as if my arms were folded up in front of my face, locked stiff and full of pins and needles: but I had no arms . . . How could my arms and legs feel cramped and trapped? They should *flow*.

It was as if my body was being squeezed and knotted into different sections like a modelling balloon, when it should be all of a piece, one smooth delta-wing. I tried to see if anything was actually happening to Semi-the-fish. But I couldn't look at myself very well, I could only see the shape of the shadow beneath me in the water. It seemed to be the same as ever.

I was so scared.

The seawater is pumped into my pool through the inflow cover. It flows out through the outflow cover. I think the inflow pipe runs together with the outflow, until it reaches underneath the pool to the other side. That would save tunnelling through the rock twice. There'll be pumping machinery, where the inflow and the outflow come out on the beach. I think that will be somewhere hidden, so there isn't any machinery showing . . . But how can I know? I'm frightened I'll push myself through the outflow, and fall into some kind of crushing, thumping, squeezing, metal hell, and then I'll die.

I'm going to die anyway. I don't want to die here, in this concrete box.

I don't want Miranda to suffer. If *my* Miranda is dead, if her human mind is gone forever, I still want to save the creature she's become. I won't let them vivisect her.

At last the dusk fell, and the tropical darkness quickly followed.

The orderly had cleaned my sluice-opening stick out of the water, but more stuff always falls in. I found another, and took it to the bottom of the pool. My useless back flippers felt different – tender and aching – but stronger, and better able to understand the peculiar human-type orders I was giving them. From what Skinner had said it seemed he had known all along there was a way out of the pool. Which meant Dr Franklin must know about it too. What did that mean? How could I tell what kind of game they were playing now? When I levered open the sluice cover again, most likely a lot of alarms would go off, spotlights would come on, and Dr Franklin would be there by the pool crying, 'Excellent! Well done, Semi!'

Or what if Skinner was really trying to help, but he didn't know? Maybe he just *hoped* that a manta ray creature the size of a flattened teenaged could wriggle down the big outflow pipe. The more I thought about it the more I remembered that Skinner was a real mess, gibbering with remorse, probably drunk too, and even if he meant well, I couldn't trust him to be thinking straight.

I had to take the risk. First chance, last chance.

Like you always said, Miranda, I thought. The next thing we try might work.

I prised open the cover, folded myself up and shoved myself into that black hole.

I don't know if I could have done it, if I hadn't been so completely desperate. But I put all my strength into that thrust: and I burst through the mouth of the outflow into a wide pipe beyond, like a cork popping out of a bottle.

The walls were smooth and slippery. I could see nothing. I was frightened that I'd come to somewhere where there was no water to breathe, and I wouldn't be able to get back. I'd keep sliding on, trapped and choking. It didn't happen. I came to the end of the straight bit, and then slithered around a bend. There was room enough, but my wings were squashed against the sides. I could hear, ahead of me, a sound like soft thunder.

A little further and the water churned around me, and I was falling.

If I'd had a voice, I would have yelled. My wings flew out wide, instinctively. I was trying to grab at the tunnel sides with the hands I didn't have. I only hurt myself, I could not get a grip. I was speeding down this steep, slippery tube, in utter blackness, faster and faster. Then I fell again! If I didn't shriek aloud that time, I certainly shrieked in my mind. But I was still gathering speed, and nothing terrible had happened to me. I could feel that I was in a bigger passageway, still full of water: it seemed to be a natural passage in the rock. I could hear a rushing noise beside me. I kept bumping into something smooth and rounded; that must be the other pipe, with the water being pumped up from the sea.

I'd known that I was going to have to descend a long way. I'd thought it would be hard work, wriggling and squeezing. Maybe this was better! I tried to think sensibly, about slowing myself down, and being prepared for new dangers, like pumping machinery or projecting rocks and other obstacles. It was impossible. In the end I just flew:

177

whoosh, splash, careering around bends and down chutes, shrieking silently but not even really afraid because it was all happening so fast. At last I fell, or I was poured with the water, over a lip of stone as sleek as polished metal. Then I was in a broader, dark channel, on the flat. There was air above the surface. I could hear machinery chugging somewhere nearby, but I managed to stay away from it.

I didn't have to worry about deciding which way to go. The force of the water pulled me onwards. I would have known the right direction, anyway. The smell of the sea, which was much more than 'smell', to my fish-senses, was overwhelming. I floated, barely swimming, still dazed and excited by my wild ride through the mountain, towards a patch of lighter darkness; it grew bigger, and I could see the blurred shapes of trees and rocks outlined against it. I could see my old friends the stars in the sky.

I drifted out onto the surface of the ocean, and lay there gazing.

I was free.

But there was something wrong.

I turned myself around and looked back. What I saw didn't make sense, until I remembered to switch some switches, and get the view in human format. Then I could see, by starlight, the trees and the swampy mangroves reaching into the water, on either side of the inlet where the pumping machinery was hidden.

Oh no. This was not the east coast.

So then I had to orient myself. There was no moon, I had to do it by the blurred stars, and by my fish-senses. I had never studied a map of the island. I vaguely remembered seeing one on the wall in Dr Franklin's office, the day we were given our lecture about genetic engineering, but I couldn't remember much about it: a blurred teardrop shape, longer on the east and west than north and south, that was all. I decided I was in the south. The sea was calm, the night was clear. All I had to do was face out to sea, turn left and swim, keeping close to the beach. Then I couldn't miss the jetty. It couldn't be more than about ten kilometres or so, nothing to Semi-the-fish.

I'd been swimming for a few minutes, before I thought about sharks.

By then, I didn't care. I was having the most magical experience of my life.

I think sharks are daylight animals, anyway.

(There's one good thing about going through horrors, you end up with a fairly casual attitude to what would once have seemed deadly danger. I had been *so terrified* the one time I saw a big shark in our lagoon, though I was standing on dry land on the coral causeway. Now I was swimming along without a care, thinking: so, a shark may come along and bite my leg off, well, accidents will happen . . .)

But I wasn't thinking about sharks with more than a very small part of my mind. Even my fear for Miranda took second place. There was nothing I could do for her at the moment except swim – and swimming through the deep blue sea, with the stars above me, was completely, totally bliss. It was wonderful, as wonderful as waking up as Semi-the-fish, the first time; only better. Everything was alive. The water was full of movement, sound and light. I try to think of how it felt in human terms, and the nearest I can come is . . . it was like swimming through music. Not loud, wild, music, not tonight: but sparkling, dancing music, with a deep steady underbeat, and distant voices weaving in and out; and I was part of this music.

I was so happy.

Miranda had never talked much about what it meant to

her to fly free. I could guess why. It would have been cruel to tell me, when I was trapped in that concrete box. Now I could understand why she had spent so much time up high, and taken such risks with that stun ring. She wasn't only gathering information, she was feeling this same joy.

Joy, that's the only word for it.

If only there was a place in the world where we could fly together—

I had no adventures, nothing attacked me. I followed the dark border of the mangroves, heading for the tip of the island – firmly resisting the tug of the great, wide ocean, that called to me from beyond the barrier reef. I had been swimming for maybe half an hour, when something strange happened: but it felt natural as breathing.

I fell asleep.

I don't know for how long I slept. Several hours, anyway.

I woke up near the surface, feeling very rested and comfortable, and naturally started swimming again. I could see the stars overhead had changed around, and it must be nearly morning. That was okay, I wasn't supposed to get to the jetty until dawn. When I'd been swimming for a few minutes, my arms came loose. Those phantom arms inside my fish-body were no longer locked in front of my phantom human face. I could move them, they were free. I was so knocked-out by the experience of swimming in the ocean, I took this easing of the locked-in feeling for granted. And then, to my total amazement, *I saw my own hands, rising beside my face. I saw my arms, smoothly pushing through the water.* The change wasn't in my mind. It was real!

My arms were free, then my legs began to kick—

Some dark stuff and some whiteish stuff streamed away

from me into the water, like a shed skin. There was no blood: which was lucky. The sharks in the lagoon would probably have woken up fast, if they smelled the blood of fresh human. Yum!

I thought I must be dreaming. How could it be this easy?

Have you ever seen a seedling, a baby weed, shoving up from under a concrete slab? Or pushing through to the sunlight, through four or five centimetres of tarmac? That's what changing was like for me, the second time. That's the power that Dr Franklin had put into his DNA infusions. That's what the chemistry of life can do.

At the time I thought maybe I'd gone crazy and I was still Semi-the-fish, having delusions caused by the antidote starting to work. Maybe it was a sign that I'd soon be helplessly twisted up in agony. Either that, or I was asleep and dreaming. But all I could do was swim on. I came up to the surface (I was swimming a few metres down) every few minutes, to check on the creamy line of the waves that rimmed the beach. I saw the sky beginning to pale with the dawn. At last I saw the jetty.

There was a small motor launch beside it. Skinner had already reached the rendezvous.

So far so good.

I dived deep, several metres deep, so I could get close to it unseen.

The water grew shallow. I was swimming along barely above the smooth, sandy bottom, by the time the hull of the boat loomed above me. I was still fish enough to have control over my buoyancy. I let myself rise very silently, and checked things out as well as I could, keeping my head underwater. There were lights in the cabin below the deck, and in the little engine house above, but I couldn't see anybody on board.

I slipped around to the stern, and scrambled up over the side.

I was breathing dry air for several breaths before I realised what I was doing. Then I panicked, and had to frantically smother a lot of gulping and choking. But there was no need to panic. I could breathe perfectly normally. I sat on the deck, gasping in silent astonishment, and felt myself all over.

What am I?

I was a soaking wet teenager, with no clothes . . . no hair, okay, and less ears than I used to have: but with toes, fingernails, teeth, everything.

Plus four pairs of raised flaps of skin, either side of my throat, that were now sealed tight, because I was breathing dry air.

I sat there happily amazed, wishing I had some clothes, wondering what I looked like with no hair, wondering what to do next.

My plan (as far as you can have a plan, when you have *no* idea what's going to happen to you) had been to reach here, and try to make sure I wasn't walking (or swimming) into a trap. If I saw any sign of those uniformed goons, or if anything else looked wrong, I'd planned to head for the open sea. Go on trying to reach Miranda by radio telepathy. Swim to the mainland, try to convince someone I was human, and come back here with a rescue party . . . Of course I hadn't meant to climb aboard Skinner's motorboat like this. I'd thought I would be Semi-the-fish. But this was much better! There didn't seem to be any goons in uniform. If Skinner was on his own, Arnie and I would easily be able to overpower him, if he had any plans to double-cross us. Then we'd use his tracking equipment to trace Miranda, we'd get her off the island and—

The truth was, the unbelievable speed and ease of the change had completely addled my brains, although I didn't realise it. I thought I was still a big strong manta ray with superpowers. I thought I could do anything! Crush that fishing boat!

I stood up, thinking *whatever it takes, I'll save you Miranda—*

I mean, I tried to stand up. Instinct had carried me when I first climbed on board. Now my legs buckled, as if I was a newborn foal. I staggered. In front of me, below the deck, the door to the cabin opened. Bright lights came on all around me.

'Excellent!' said Doctor Franklin. 'Well done, Semi!'

I tried to jump for the side. I fell over. He leapt up the steps, grabbed me by the arm, and half carried me, half hustled me into the cabin.

Skinner was there. He was sitting on a swivel chair, facing us. Behind him was a computer keyboard. The computer's monitor screen showed blue sea, with a map of what must be Dr Franklin's island. I could still see as clearly as Semi-the-fish. I could see all the details, the contour lines on the land and the charted waters of the ocean. I stared at Skinner. I was disgusted with myself for trusting him . . . but then I realised that while Dr Franklin was holding my arm with one hand (I wasn't trying to struggle) in his other hand he was holding a gun. He was pointing it at Skinner.

'You're a madman Charlie,' he said. 'You may have had a romantic idea of rescue, but you should at least have been waiting for her by the pump outlet. What if she'd taken off for the open sea? She could have been very expensive sharkmeat by now.'

Dr Skinner was staring at me in amazement. 'I thought

you'd be suspicious,' he whispered. 'I was supposed to be on patrol. I had to take the risk. I thought—'

'You took a good many risks,' said Dr Franklin, 'It's lucky I found out what you were doing. Oh Charlie, Charlie, did you think you could get away with it?' Then he laughed. 'But never mind. I was in control. I am always prepared.' He beamed at me, his eyes glittering with delight. 'This is, my, my, a most unexpected pleasure, Semirah. Wonderful, superb! Not quite what I had planned, but never mind! I can't wait to get you back to the lab. Charlie, you are forgiven.'

But where's Arnie? I thought. What happened to Arnie? Is he dead then? Was he dead all along? Delayed shock was hitting me. My legs were made of jelly, my head was full of cotton wool. I started to choke. Something hard was caught in my throat. I couldn't think what it was. Manta rays don't swallow objects, it must have been in there since I was last a girl. I doubled over, retching, and the thing shot out of my mouth, with a rush of seawater.

Dr Skinner groaned, and dropped his head into his hands.

Dr Franklin tucked his gun away. It was clear that Dr Skinner wasn't going to put up any kind of a fight. He said smugly, 'I'll take that. There's a great deal of valuable information stored on that chip.' He stooped and swept up the tag I'd been carrying around with me, inside my body. As soon as he let go of my arm, I collapsed. I stared up into those cold, bright, self-satisfied eyes. I was human again, but I knew that what Dr Franklin saw was still an animal, a thing to be used. That was the way he saw everyone but himself. Something icy and piercing struck my arm. In seconds I was unconscious.

When I woke up, the sun was hot on my face. I tried to get

my arms free, but I couldn't. I opened my eyes. I was back in the enclosure. I was in a wheelchair, on the gravel path beside the pool. They'd put me into pyjamas and strapped me into a straitjacket again.

Dr Franklin had warned us it would happen, if we didn't behave.

He was there. So was Skinner, and some orderlies. The tracking equipment I'd seen on the boat was there too, on a metal trolley. I stared at the beautifully clear and detailed monitor screen, thinking numbly: Arnie's dead and Miranda's gone. Were they going to lock me up again and leave me? I imagined myself living in here among the bushes. The orderly would bring food and dump it on the ground, and I'd eat it with my hands.

'Ah, you're awake,' said Dr Franklin. He had a big grin on his face. 'You've done very, very well, Semi. Many congratulations! I'm delighted with your performance in Dr Skinner's little "escape attempt" exercise, hahaha! I only wish I'd thought of it myself.'

He looked like a middle-aged little boy with a new lego set.

'Soon I'm going to get you into the lab, young woman. Your response to the second stage infusion is beyond my hopes, I'm absolutely thrilled. There is major investigation to be done: I want to biopsy the internal organs and the brain, take samples of your spinal fluid, oh, there are years of work!'

I wouldn't let myself scream. I knew he wouldn't care one way or the other, but it was for my own pride. I couldn't bear to look at Skinner. I could see him out of the corner of my eye, polishing his glasses with trembling hands. What happened to you? I wanted to yell at him. But I could guess. Dr Franklin had found out something about Skinner's plans, and forced the miserable coward to tell him the rest.

Poor Charlie!

Maybe I shouldn't have pitied him, but I did.

I was going to be tortured to death. But I still felt as if I'd rather be me than him.

I looked at Dr Franklin. I knew it didn't matter what I said. I was nothing more than a rat in his maze. I said it anyway. 'I'm glad Miranda got away. You can't hurt her now.'

I knew she hadn't escaped from the island. Or from the horror that was our future. I meant her mind had escaped, forever. He could hurt the bird-monster, and that was bad. But better to be a monster, than to be a prisoner on this island and have a human mind.

'I suppose you mean emotional pain,' said Dr Franklin, cheerfully. 'Which I'm afraid can't be avoided in your case. I'm afraid you are both bound to suffer some discomfort in the next phase of my research, but I will cause as little physical pain as possible. I am never needlessly cruel! *However* . . . you may be interested to learn that Miranda is actually back with us. She had been seen circling over the compound. That's why you're here. I've decided, seeing the way you have responded to the second infusion, that I want her back under close observation, right now. I don't want to use the stun ring, that would be harsh . . . so we're going to leave you here for a while. I'm afraid you have to be under restraint, after the way you've behaved, but that may be all to the good. If Miranda can recognise that her friend is in trouble, that may bring her in.' He gestured towards the orderlies. I saw the net, the long spiked poles. One of them was carrying a rifle.

I choked back a cry of protest. I knew it would do no good.

'Oh, don't worry, we're not going to injure her. The rifle fires tranquilliser darts. Now we'd better get out of sight,' Dr Franklin went on. 'It would help if you would call her up on your radio link. She may no longer be able to understand or respond consciously, but I believe it will have an effect.'

I stared at him, and shook my head.

Our creator frowned. 'Semi, Miranda's loss is a blow to me too. Of course, I knew that I was making her psychological survival more difficult: by making her my favourite and then abandoning her, by giving her the ability to fly, and then giving her partial freedom. I had to test my transgenics to the limit. Naturally I made things harder for Miranda: because she seemed the stronger of the two of you. But that doesn't mean I'm not *sorry*. Now please be sensible and co-operate, so that I don't have to hurt her. Don't you want to know if she still remembers you?'

I told him what he could do with the idea that I would betray my friend.

He shrugged, his eyes bright and cool. He wasn't angry. 'Resistant to the last. Well done! It doesn't matter, we can fake your call sign.' He nodded to Dr Skinner.

Skinner obediently put on a headset, and did some tapping on the computer keyboard.

I started to struggle, hopelessly but furiously. I shouted at Skinner, 'How can you do this? He's mad, but you're not mad! How can you let things like this happen! Help me!'

Skinner winced as if he could hear the jungle cat howling, but he wouldn't look at me. He said to Dr Franklin, 'I'm picking up a response. She's coming in again.'

Dr Franklin spoke to the orderlies in Spanish. They

moved off, under the trees. He stayed where he was, staring at the sky.

'Ha! There she is! How splendidly she flies!'

I could see the black T-shape of Miranda flying low. She was zooming in fast over the science buildings. Then I *did* call her up. There was nothing to be gained from keeping quiet now. I called her name, I yelled silently, *Miranda! Get away from here! It's a trap!* There was no answer, no sense of her presence in my mind. It all felt blank, blanker than the white place. I screamed at her, aloud, 'Get away from here! Get away from here!' Dr Franklin turned to me, with an exasperated expression—

'Semi, please!'

Then Miranda was gone. She'd vanished.

'Where's she gone!' exclaimed Dr Franklin, 'She saw us! Is she flying away again?'

'No,' said Skinner. 'No . . . She's close, don't know where, too many buildings—'

I started shouting again, for what good it would do: 'Miranda, fly! *Go away,* it's a trap!'

Everyone, including the orderlies with their big net and their prodding poles, was looking this way and that: where had she gone? Then as suddenly as she'd disappeared she was there again. She was overhead, she was diving into the enclosure. Her wings looked huge. She swooped into the mango tree and crouched on a branch: a monster out of a scary legend, winged and bird-headed, but human enough to horrify.

Her beak opened in a fierce, harsh cry—

'Aha!' exclaimed Dr Franklin. 'Excellent! *Now* what, I wonder . . . ?' He added something in Spanish. The orderlies moved in on the mango tree, slowly and cautiously.

I shouted, 'Miranda! Get out of here!' I thought she didn't know me. She wasn't my friend Miranda. She was a weird wild animal, obeying vague memories that she no longer understood . . . That's what I thought. The bird-monster turned her head from side to side, fixing Dr Franklin with a fierce, empty glare. Then she bent down, and very deliberately tore at the black bracelet on her ankle with her razor sharp beak.

She had it off in about two seconds, and glared at us again, defiantly.

I understood she could always have done that. But she had stayed with me.

'Oh Miranda,' I whispered. 'You could have flown away. You could have brought back help. You could have saved us both. Why didn't you?'

Then I thought, *that's not a monster, that's Miranda again!*

Even though I knew what horrors awaited us, my heart leapt for joy—

'Excellent!' cried Dr Franklin, almost clapping his hands. 'Oh, excellent, Miranda!'

The orderlies didn't think this development was so excellent. They bunched closer together, nervously holding out their poles. They didn't seem keen to get close enough to fling the net. She was a bird as big as a golden eagle, with a fierce beak and razor sharp talons, and wings strong enough to break a man's arm if she got a good swipe at him. And she wasn't looking in a good temper.

While they hesitated, something was happening in Dr Franklin's zoo. The noise from that courtyard had been steadily growing. Now it was a confused roar of squealing and grunting. A horde of weird animals poured into view, racing out from between the nearby buildings: the capybara, the wild pigs, the parrots and the bats flapping overhead; others I hadn't seen before. It looked like some kind of weird hallucination: a hideous, freakish mob, all of them running crazy with panic and sudden freedom.

'What in hell—!' yelled Dr Franklin.

'She's let them out!' I shouted, 'Miranda let them out!'

Miranda leapt from her perch, and flew at Dr Franklin's face, talons outspread—

The orderlies started yelling. Dr Franklin struggled with Miranda on the edge of the pool. I saw his face slashed red, I saw him rolling on the ground, beaten around the head by blows from her wings. Transgenic animals were racing round the enclosure, squealing. It was pandemonium. I was screaming madly, *Leave him! They've got a gun! Fly away!* Dr Franklin fell into the water. He was floundering and gasping – it seemed the mad scientist couldn't swim. Some of the orderlies were trying to reach him, some were trying to throw the net over Miranda. She was stabbing at eyes and clawing at faces, shrieking, flying free of the net and the rods—

Something hit my chair. I wasn't strapped in: I went flying. I couldn't save myself, my arms were wrapped up and fastened at the back by the straps of the straitjacket. I hit the gravel with a thump, folded arms first, winded. Someone stooped over me, I felt a tug. A voice hissed in my ear: *'head for the jetty, the launch is still there—'* . . . and then Dr Skinner was on his feet, running to join the others. He didn't look back.

Miranda had taken flight, but the net was tangled around her, hampering her wings. Dr Franklin was out of the pool. All the men were running after Miranda, Skinner with them, and Dr Franklin, soaking wet. He was shouting, *'Get a dart into her! Fire as soon as you have a clear shot!'* The restraint on my arms had gone slack. Skinner had unfastened the straps at my back. I struggled free of the jacket. The enclosure was empty. I ran, (I mean I staggered and stumbled, my legs were very wobbly) to the gate. Oh no. It was on a spring, it had shut and locked itself behind the men when they'd rushed through. No! I thought. *I will not be beaten!* I looked up at the fence and knew I couldn't climb it.

Something flashed into my mind.

Those patterns that Miranda used to make and break up—

The one pattern that she had *made sure* I would see.

We had been stuck in here, me making my plans, and she making her own, with no way to share our secrets. But I caught on fast. Miranda had released the animals, by opening their locked cages. She must have learned the code for this keypad as well. She could have opened our cage any time, the same as she could have pulled off that ring.

If there'd been any point. If I could have got away—

Five seedpods. Six red flower petals. Three manky pieces of melon rind, nine sticks, two dead butterflies. Five, six, three, nine, two. I slipped my hand through the mesh, reached for the keypad on the lock, and tapped in the code. It took me a couple of times. I was drenched in sweat. My fingers slipped off the keys, and they weren't . . . they were out of the habit of *being* fingers. But I did it. The lock clicked, I was out. Leaving the noise of the chase somewhere behind me, I set off at a stumbling trot for the science blocks.

It was bad to be inside those buildings again. Even the

coolness of the air-conditioning reminded me of terror. The operating theatre must be somewhere near here: the place where we'd been given our infusions. The place where our evil creator would take Miranda, and me too, and torture us again, if we couldn't save ourselves. I opened door after door. Empty, bright, clinical rooms. I found a walk-in cold cupboard with stacked shelves, but everything was general science supplies, genetic-engineering chemicals in packets and tubs; pieces of animals in plastic jars. I found a chest freezer, full of opaque white boxes holding who knows what horrors, but everything in there was heavily crusted with ice and it was obvious that nothing had been touched for a long time. At last I found an ordinary looking kitchen fridge, standing on a counter in a long thin room full of other, stranger machinery. The label on the door said, Transgenic Project H.

H for human?

I looked inside, and found two stacks of small white boxes.

One of the stacks was labelled S, one was labelled M.

I started opening the boxes. I found little vials of blood, of clear fluid, little gobbets of tissue. Everything was dated. These must be samples taken from me and from Miranda, at different stages of our treatment. In the last of the boxes labelled S, I found more of those tubes of powder. The label said Infusion Stage B. No date.

I scrabbled through Miranda's boxes, and found *her* Infusion Stage B.

No tubes of powder. A hypodermic, and glistening ampoules of pale fluid.

That explains why she couldn't be dosed sneakily, like me, I thought. Someone has to give her injections. My heart sank. How would I know what to do? How much to give her at once? But there was no time to worry about it. There was a lab coat hanging on the back of a door. I grabbed it, spread it out and tumbled boxes into it, the two labelled Infusion B and as many others as I could grab. I didn't know what might be useful. I'd tied this bundle round my waist and I was about to leave, when I saw there was another stack of white boxes, behind our two. Each of them had a taped initial and a date, too.

The initial was A.

There was an Infusion B box, with the initial A.

Arnie?

But Arnie's dead, I thought.

The way Dr Franklin and Skinner had behaved didn't make sense, if they'd really had someone reporting on our conversations. Dr Franklin hadn't seemed to know if his radio telepathy was working properly or not. Dr Skinner had talked about brain-waves, but he'd been shocked when he saw me prove that I was still human inside. It all pointed to things being the way Arnie had told us. The doctors could detect brain-activity in our speech centres, but they didn't know what we were saying. They weren't sure if we were saying anything human. But, wait, it was Arnie who had told us that.

Arnie?

I tugged the bundle from my waist, unfastened it, swept the A boxes in there and tied it up again. I didn't clearly know why I was doing that, but it seemed I must. I was wondering whether I should try to do some random vandalism, or should I get out of here. I was going to call Miranda, and I hoped and prayed she would answer me this time.

But someone called me first.

No, he didn't call me. I had been calling his name, in my

mind, strongly enough to make contact: and he was answering me. *Semi? Semi? Hey, Hey, SEMI?*

It was Arnie. And he was somewhere close by.

12

It's a trap, I thought.

So near to escape. I couldn't bear to stop now.

Don't trust anyone on this island, I thought. They're all working for Dr Franklin.

Semi, Semi . . . called the voice in my mind, getting desperate, and it sounded like Arnie. Not a fake. It sounded to me like that annoying, sarcastic, lonely boy—

I didn't answer. I was afraid to trust my instincts. But I couldn't leave without looking for him. I didn't have *time* for this, and I was terrified it was another trap, but I couldn't help myself. I didn't know my way around the science blocks, but I came to a corridor I recognised, and from there it was easy. There was no one around, no one at all. Everyone must be out in the courtyards, chasing after all those escaped animals . . . and Miranda. The building with the prison ward in it wasn't locked today. I found my way to the corridor outside that room with the beds surrounded by bars.

The door was locked.

So it was no use. If Arnie was in there, I'd have to leave him.

But wait, wait. There was something I knew, something I remembered!

In a bad situation, gather information and hang on to it if

you can. Anything you find out may be useful. Thank you Miranda, for telling me that! I quickly found that panel in the wall that I'd seen Skinner open, the night he tried to help us escape. It slid aside. I switched off the prison ward's security system. The door to the ward came open when I pushed it. It was a thick, heavy door. As soon as it moved, I could hear something inside the room thumping and banging, like a big animal.

All the doors to the cages were standing open. I'd released all the locks. In the one cage that wasn't empty, I saw something limbless and gleaming, strapped to a steel bed frame. It was thick as my waist, and folded up in a figure of eight. It looked huge. It had a pattern of darker scales along the sides of its pale body, and a cap of wires strapped to its head. There was a computer and a monitor screen and some other high-tech hospital machinery on a workstation table. The snake was writhing furiously, fighting against heavy-duty flexible bands that held it down.

Its large golden eyes stared at me, the pupils slits of fury. Its mouth, a reptilian line without lips or teeth, was gaping, a choked hissing sound came from its throat. There was nothing, *nothing* I could recognise. You couldn't tell it had ever been human.

'Arnie?' I whispered, forgetting I didn't need to speak aloud. 'Is that *you*, Arnie?'

'*Get me out of here!*' howled the voice in my mind—

'Okay, okay, I'll try!'

The snake had stopped fighting, as soon as I spoke its human name. It gave a sort of long sigh. The golden eyes stared, showing no emotion. The voice in my mind said: 'You'll have to switch off the setup, or you'll kill me if you try to get the wires off my head. Do what I say. Don't make any stupid mistakes, okay?'

196

I tapped the keys, as he told me. Then I went up to the bed. I couldn't help hesitating.

What if I killed him? What if he killed me? This could be another trap.

'Semi,' gasped the voice in my head, 'it is me. I'm in here. *Please*—'

'What if I kill you?'

'Choice between that and staying strapped up like this, it's *not a big worry*!'

So I unfastened the bands that held the cap, and pulled it off him. He was okay. We both breathed a sigh of relief. As quickly as I could with my fumbling new-born hands, I released the straps that held him to the frame. Arnie-the-snake *exploded* off the bed, coiled himself and struck at the bedframe, at the cap of wires, at that stack of computer equipment. It didn't take him any time at all to reduce the lot to twisted metal and plastic rubble. He was immensely strong. If Miranda was built for the air, and me for the ocean, this transgenic human had been built for earth and rock. He flowed like lava.

He was *very* scary.

'What's the matter?' demanded Arnie, in my head – his animal body rearing up so he could look into my face – 'I didn't like those machines, anything wrong with that?'

'Nothing!' I gasped, 'N-nothing! Arnie, Miranda's in the compound.' I didn't know how much he knew of what had been going on. 'She flew away, but she's come back. She let the animals out, as a diversion, but they're all after her, they're going to catch her.'

'Come on then, let's go!' Arnie-the-snake dropped to the floor and shot away. I stumbled after him. We hurried down the corridors, following the same route as when Dr Skinner had tried to help Miranda and I to escape; and

197

reached the door to the zoo courtyard. Dr Franklin's zoo was a mess. There were orderlies trying to round up the animals. The capybara with the human eyes and lips was blundering about, shaking its head. Parrots with the tattered human hands among their breast feathers were flying around screeching wildly. The bats with the human legs fluttered and twittered, free but miserable in the sunlight. Piglets were running, squealing. The big wild sow was at bay in a corner between two buildings, a couple of fallen bodies in uniform suggesting she'd already fought off one attack. Some deer with strange looking heads were galloping about. No sign of Miranda, no sign of Skinner or Dr Franklin. No one had spotted us yet.

'What'll we do?' gasped Arnie.

'I don't know! Skinner said "head for the jetty". I think the motor launch is still there—'

'*Skinner*!' Arnie-the-snake's golden eyes glared at me. 'Do you trust him?'

Then, with a flurry like wings, Miranda was there in our minds.

'Hey, you two! Get out of the compound! The boat is still there! Look after yourselves, I'm okay, I'll meet you at the boat!'

Which way should we run? In a moment we'd be spotted. My head was spinning, there were black dots in front of my eyes, and suddenly I knew I wasn't going to run anywhere. My legs were about to fold under me.

'Arnie, I can't do it. You'll have to go without me.'

'What's up with you?' he snapped. Typical sympathetic Arnie.

'I just went through the change again. It was easier, but it takes it out of you.'

'Oh yeah. You're human again. I getcha. It was tough

work, huh?' His snake head whipped to and fro. 'Can you drive?' said the voice in my mind.

'Uh, what good . . . I can drive a quad bike, I suppose—'

'Then we're in business!'

The electric cart the orderlies used for delivering food to the animals was standing near the doorway where we were lurking. I jumped into it, Arnie-the-snake flowing up beside me. The key was in the ignition. The cart started up.

Then Arnie shouted, 'Wait! Stop!'

It was weird to see those expressionless reptilian eyes, and hear his human voice.

'Something I've got to do.'

Arnie dropped from the cab and shot across the ground, to where a bunch of the uniformed orderlies were bending over something wrapped in netting. The men were too amazed to react. The thing under the net was the jungle cat. It was lying still, its eyes wide open, staring out of its endless, hopeless pain. Miranda had opened its cage, but it was still imprisoned. Arnie coiled himself and lashed out, smashing its tortured head with a single blow of his tail. The orderlies stood gaping. Arnie zoomed back to me.

'Sorry, but I had to do that. I could hear it, all this time. Had to set it free.'

'You were right.'

We went careering away, scattering deer, capybara, piglets. Some of the orderlies spotted us and gave chase, shouting, but we were well ahead of them when we came out of the buildings on to the open ground. Now there was no cover between us and the tall perimeter fence. I didn't know how I was going to get down that steep track, but we weren't done for yet. I gripped the wheel of the little cart, gunning it as fast as it would go, but that wasn't very fast. We seemed to be driving through treacle, moving incredibly slowly. I could see the gate. I was heading straight for it. On either side of me, I could see two of the big jeeps converging. I realised that we weren't going to make it . . .

'Come on! Come on!' yelled Arnie.

The foremost jeep swerved in front of me and thundered to a halt. Uniformed men poured out of it. I flung the wheel around . . . and there was the other jeep. I tried to put the cart in reverse, but I couldn't find reverse. The cart jolted to a halt.

The electric motor whined and died. I covered my face with my hands.

'Well,' said Dr Franklin's voice, a little out of breath. 'This has been exciting!'

I wanted to die. I uncovered my face, and saw more of Dr Franklin's men coming through the gate in the fence. They had Miranda in a net. Two of them were carrying her, several others were close on either side, prodding her with their rods. She was fighting, shrieking, striking out with her beak and talons as well as she could.

Dr Skinner was with his boss. Give him credit, he looked pretty sickened.

When she saw that we'd been recaptured, Miranda went quiet.

One of the orderlies put the padlock back on the gate and locked it. Dr Franklin took out a remote control, and pressed some buttons. He spoke to the men who were carrying Miranda, and they hurriedly moved away from the tall fence.

I could *feel* Arnie-the-snake beside me, calculating how many of them he could take out, before they would gun him down.

'Arnie,' I called to him silently. 'Don't do it. You'll make things worse.'

'How so?' said Arnie-the-snake. 'What would be worse?'

'I've got an idea. We'll go to the white place. You and me and Miranda. We can hide in our own minds, and he won't be able to hurt us. It'll be like being dead.'

But the white place had always been a tricky sort of illusion. It wouldn't come. I couldn't make the leap, and I couldn't pull Miranda and Arnie along with me. I was too tired, too defeated. I couldn't escape that way. I saw Dr Franklin staring at me and Arnie. I saw his gaze moving over Miranda, who was lying there in the net, the uniformed men ready to jab her if she moved. I could see his frustration. He had made us, but he didn't know what was going on in our minds.

That was what frightened him. Not Miranda's talons or Arnie's massive strength. He'd created us, but he didn't understand us, and for him that was unbearable. I was glad, bitterly glad, that we'd got to him. But I knew there'd be a horrible price to pay.

'Dr Skinner,' he said, briskly, 'I think we'll remove the brain implants straight away. The radio telepathy idea needs much more work, there's no point in letting the trial continue. Miranda, since I gather you are with us again, in spirit, as it were, I'm afraid you are going to have to stay in that net until you are safely confined. Semi is looking very tired. I'm going to return you all to the ward, at once.'

Miranda shrieked.

Arnie's voice in my mind muttered something like, *Semi, what about it*—?

I answered something like *yes*, and we charged. I'd run out of plans, I'd run out of ideas. We were not going back to that ward with the bars round the beds. We were not going to be vivisected. There was nothing, *nothing* else to do but go out in a blaze of glory. Arnie's glittering muscular body shot into the bunch of orderlies around Miranda, like a battering ram. Three of them went down like ninepins. The rest scattered, yelling. I flung myself on the net, scrabbling to get it off her. The men in uniform didn't know what to do. A couple of them got out their guns, real guns, and started waving them and shouting. They didn't seem to have an idea what was going on, but they were still obeying orders, trying to get us back to the ward. Anyone who tried to grab me, got slammed by Arnie's tail. Dr Franklin was shouting in Spanish. I don't know what Skinner was doing. The orderlies had Arnie down, a whole bunch of them on his back; meanwhile I had freed Miranda. She shrieked at me, but I could see the human Miranda looking out of the bird-monster's eyes, and I was happy.

She could have flown away then, only she wouldn't leave us. There was blood on her wing feathers, but she wasn't hurt badly. She launched herself into the air, and came screaming back, her great wings thundering. One of the uniformed men had my arms behind my back. I think he was trying not to hurt me, because I was a girl, not a weird animal, but he was struggling hard to get a jab at my neck or my arm, with some kind of hypodermic. I was struggling and screaming. Miranda was beating at my attacker with her wings. Arnie had burst free from the men who'd been holding him down, and was coiling himself for a new attack . . . I heard Dr Franklin shouting, '*No!* Don't shoot to kill! Don't damage them! I want them alive! *I haven't finished with them!*'

He had the tranquilliser dart rifle. He was levelling it at Miranda—

The next things happened very slowly.

Arnie lunged at Dr Franklin, slapped the rifle aside, and hit him a tremendous blow, right in his face. It lifted him off the ground. He sailed into the air like a rag doll, blood pouring from his nose. Miranda caught the rifle in her talons and yanked it away from him, swinging him around. Dr Franklin went flying, twisting, his spine slamming against the mesh of the electrified fence—

Everyone stood still, paralysed with shock. Dr Franklin jerked a bit and then he was just hanging there, his neck all crooked, blood on his face, a smell of scorching coming from his clothes. I think I heard him muttering, '*Excellent, well done, very resilient . . .*'

But I expect I imagined that.

Dr Skinner said, in a strange, flat voice, 'Better switch off the juice and get him down.' The men looked at him blankly. He said it again, in Spanish (I suppose).

I'd collapsed in a heap on the ground. I was crying. Not for Dr Franklin, no way. I was crying out of pure stress and exhaustion; and a dull sort of feeling that was the nearest I could come to incredible relief.

The men were all taken up with Dr Franklin, getting him down, deciding he was really dead. They took no notice of us; the two weird animals and the sobbing girl.

About an hour later we were on the motor launch. Semi the former fish, Miranda-the-bird perched on the rail; and Arnie-the-snake coiled up on the foredeck (taking up most of the space, it wasn't a big boat). Dr Skinner didn't say much, when he saw us off. He'd given us the instructions to go with Infusion Stage B, and made sure I knew how to use a hypodermic. But he hadn't tried to argue with me, when I'd said we'd didn't want his help, and we wanted to leave at once. He was in no state to argue with anyone. According to the charts, it was only about forty kilometres to the mainland, and I'm an island girl (at least in the summer holidays). I thought I could manage.

He said 'Good luck,' and he walked away.

We looked at each other in silence, two monsters and one human being in green hospital-type pyjamas, with no hair and gills in her neck. It seemed like a long, long way from the beach where we'd been prisoners in paradise.

'Let's get out to sea first,' said Miranda's voice in my mind.

I suppose the mental switches were being flipped, but we were so used to our radio telepathy that making contact could happen automatically, like walking into a dark room and reaching for the light switch. It was exactly like talking.

'Are you sure you can do this?' said Arnie worriedly.

'Drive a motor boat?' I said, scornfully. 'Please. I've been in boats all my life. As long as we have enough fuel: and I think we do.'

So I cast off and started up the motor, and we set out, heading east.

When we were beyond the reef, I cut the engine.

I said, 'We should check the supplies.'

Arnie coiled himself up and muttered that he was feeling tired out. Miranda-the-bird and I opened lockers and peered into corners. We had charts. We had cans of extra petrol, a good supply of drinking water; we had biscuits and tinned food. Dr Skinner had been prepared for a getaway before Dr Franklin had interupted his plans, and he'd made sure he had plenty of stuff. We would be okay. Miranda and I ripped out all the wiring, computer and radio equipment, and chucked it over the side. That was reckless, but even though we'd seen Dr Franklin dead, and Dr Skinner had let us go, we weren't taking any chances. We'd rather be lost at sea than back on that island.

When all this was done, we rejoined Arnie. Together we went to the white place. I was half aware of the boat and the heading we were on, but I was with the others too, in that spooky white cloud.

'I could've got the ring off,' said Miranda. 'I could have flown away. I didn't dare. I was afraid he'd kill you, Semi. To hide the evidence, in case I managed to come back with the police.'

'Franklin was going to test you to destruction,' said Arnie. 'He'd prepared the second stage infusions, but he wasn't really interested in changing us back. Not until he'd finished playing his games, anyway. He had me wired up, the way Semi saw. He had Miranda ringed, and Semi had the tag in her stomach, that she didn't know about. He wanted to see how you two stood up to isolation. He planned that you would both escape, or at least try and escape, and he'd observe what happened. He had the fantasy that you were like transgenic astronauts, surviving with no human contact on an alien planet, and if you both died or lost your minds, that would be okay. He was prepared to *sacrifice* one of you or both of you, as a step on the way to creating superhumans. He reckoned he'd be learning how to do better next time. He didn't know he wasn't going to be able to listen-in on the radio link he'd given us. That was a setback, but he decided to carry on, using me as his control.

'He wanted you to believe I was still human, to make you feel more isolated. He said that if I told you I'd been changed, *he would never change us back.* I didn't know how much he could tell from reading those brain-wave print-outs. I didn't dare to risk it. All I could do was tell you not to escape. And rely on Skinner.' Arnie shuddered. 'You know, Franklin always talked to me as if I was human, when I was changed. But I could see in his eyes that he didn't believe it. I was just a thing.'

'In a way,' I said, 'It was good that he decided to play those mind-games. That was what broke Skinner. He was prepared to go along with the great work, otherwise, even when it meant torturing and nearly murdering three teenagers. He worshipped Franklin. In a horrible, horrible way, I can see why.'

'Dr Franklin was an evil man,' said Miranda softly. 'And he was crazy as a bedbug. But he was a genius.'

Arnie and I couldn't argue with that.

We compared notes over again, this time with Arnie telling the truth, and worked out that he must have gone through the change more or less at the same time as the two of us. The dubious honour of being first human transgenic was divided between Miranda and Arnie, and we'd never know who had actually been first across the line.

When we'd talked ourselves out, we flipped the mental switches and came back to the boat. I took out the two white boxes marked A and M, Infusion B. I spread Dr Skinner's idiot-proof instructions on the deck, and laid out the hypodermics and the ampoules.

I said, 'Are you sure you want to do this now?'

'I'm sure,' said Miranda's voice, in my mind.

'Me too,' said Arnie. 'This suit is great for weaponry, but I want my stupid body back.'

'Don't you think we should wait? Until we're back in civilisation?'

Arnie shrugged his glittering coils, 'Infusion B worked okay on you.'

Miranda said, 'The stuff was being stored cold. If we wait

until we get to a hospital, and until we've explained everything, it might be spoiled. There's another thing, Semi. I want to be changed back before anyone sees us. I don't trust *any* grown ups right now, not even my own Mum and Dad. I don't want to end up in some kind of official, legal, well-meaning Dr Franklin's lab, being taken apart to see how I work.'

'I agree,' said Arnie. 'Wonder Girl is right on the money. For once.'

The snake-monster and the bird-monster gave each other a long, hard stare: Miranda turning her head to and fro, bird-style, to give him the benefit of both sides; Arnie's lidless eyes having to manage without any form of expression.

'There were some things I handled badly,' said Miranda, at last.

'Some things I handled badly too,' said Arnie. 'Call it quits, Wonder Girl?'

'Say you'll stop calling me Wonder Girl?'

'No. I'm going to go on calling you Wonder Girl, when you deserve it.'

Miranda shrugged. 'Oh, okay. Call it quits.'

So then I read the instructions about a million times, and finally got up the nerve to inject Arnie. He wanted to be first. I gave him the full dose that he needed, for the second phase of the transgenesis. We had discussed breaking up the treatment, to make the effect more gradual. But Dr Skinner had said it would be okay doing it in one go, and we were worried about the infusion spoiling in the heat. I had to inject him in the back of the neck, into the spinal fluid. There was a piece of sticky plastic film, that I had to line up with the pattern on his scales, to mark where the needle should go in. I was scared; but it wasn't hard. Dr Skinner had told me about squirting a little bit of the fluid out first, so I didn't put any air bubbles into Arnie's blood. Or whatever it was he used for blood, in that strange body. Arnie's needle was a monster, with a pump attachment. It had to be tough to get through his skin. But he didn't make any fuss.

Then we talked for a few minutes, about the odd details of being transgenic. Like, my eyesight seemed to be permanently corrected; but on the other hand, Arnie couldn't read in his snake body. Everything he'd learned about what was going on, he'd memorised from what the two mad scientists told him, or said to each other when they were near him. Miranda said she doubted if this reluctant-reader thing was a big change . . . but she said it in a friendly way. Arnie's voice started to get drowsy. He curled up tight on the floor of the boat and mumbled, in our heads, 'I am now going to sink into a deep, reptilian torpor, and shed my skin. Have a large cheeseburger and fries ready, for when I wake up.'

We watched the snake body, pulsing, gently, rhythmically. He was asleep.

'My turn,' said Miranda.

I injected four ampoules of the clear fluid, right over her breastbone. I don't think Arnie's injections hurt him at all. I think one of the things Dr Franklin was trying for, when he made the Arnie-monster, was a high resistance to any kind of pain. I had to hurt Miranda, and that was hard, but I did it. She got down from the railing for the injections. When they were done she fluffed up her feathers and settled with her legs tucked under her, like a bird on its nest. I sat beside her.

I couldn't hold her hand, because she had no hands, but I stroked her feathers. I told her a little more about my adventures; and she told me about hers.

'But why did you fly away in the end?' I asked. 'I was so scared!'

'I don't know,' said Miranda, 'That was real, Semi. I was *losing myself.* Especially after you had the antidote, and I didn't. There was a while when I didn't know who I was or where I was. But I remembered you.' She closed her eyes, and opened them again. 'Semi, I'm starting to feel very strange. I think I can't . . . talk . . . any more.'

Her eyes closed, and didn't open. I sat in Dr Franklin's motor boat, the blue ocean all around me, the blue sky above. Her voice murmured faintly in my mind—

'Exciting, a great adventure—'

Say it, Semi—

Then I waited, to see what would happen.

13

Day One Hundred and Eighty-Eight.
Two weeks later, two teenage girls were sitting on the beds in a hotel room in Quito.

Sunlight through the balcony curtains, the sound of people chatting by the poolside.

Arnie had left us. His parents had flown to Ecuador to pick him up as soon as they got the news. Miranda and I were expecting my mum, and Miranda's Mum and Dad. They were travelling together. We were waiting for a phone call from reception, to tell us the car was ready, that would take us to the airport to meet them.

I had spent five days alone on that boat, while Arnie changed and Miranda changed: keeping them covered up from the sun, watching over their bodies. I had let the boat drift for most of that time, using the engine only when the compass in the enginehouse said we were straying from our course. They had needed no food or water while the change was going on, and my appetite was tiny. I wasn't used to eating like a human. But there'd been no risk of us running out of supplies. There's plenty of water in raw fish, and there were plenty of fish about, in the sunlit layers, without any idea of what to do when a speedy, amphibious predator *with hands* came after them.

I could still breathe in water at that time, easy as breathing in dry air.

When Arnie changed back, he was very fat. They had bulked him up before they changed him into the snake, to get the raw material for all that solid transgenic muscle. But the bulk vanished, amazingly fast. We had a couple of setbacks (due to freaky weather, nothing wrong with my navigation!). By the time we ended up on the coast of Ecuador, he looked normal and we were almost as thin as we'd ever been. We were dressed even worse than we'd been as castaways. I had my hospital pyjamas, Arnie and Miranda had to make do with Flintstone clothing made out of the sacking I'd been using as a sunshade, which I'd found in one of the lockers. We hadn't thought of clothes before we left the island. Everything had happened in such a rush.

We reached the place called Menozes in the back of a friendly farmer's truck. We had no money, so he took us to some nuns who ran an orphanage outside the town. Not taking any chances, we called up Miranda's parents, straightaway. They called the British Embassy in Quito. The nuns were okay, but we did not feel safe until we'd been picked up and flown to the capital, well away from Dr Franklin's former kingdom. It was only when we got to Quito that we discovered that we'd been missing for nearly six months. We'll never work out how the count of days got so far off, and we don't much care. It doesn't matter. The notch-cutting ceremony was worthwhile anyway. It was one of our greatest inventions.

The story is, we were the lone survivors of the plane crash. Our liferaft carried us to an outlying atoll, where we lived until we were discovered by the friendly staff of Dr George Franklin's private research station, when they went cruising by one day on a fishing trip. Dr Skinner was having serious problems, due to his boss's accidental death, and the mechanical failure of the research station's helicopter and their two small planes. Oh, and the island's telecommunications had been disabled by an electrical storm. So he couldn't contact anyone, and we got impatient. We 'borrowed' a motor launch and took off by ourselves. Stupid teenagers, no sense of responsibility. We were lucky we reached the mainland unharmed.

It's not a very good story, but it's worked so far.

Of course people will come looking. Someday soon, planes and boats and helicopters will descend on Dr Franklin's island. They'll want to know why Dr Franklin and Dr Skinner didn't know that the Planet Savers' plane went down so near their base. All the parents and families of the people who died, and the aviation authorities, will want a full investigation. Arnie and Miranda and I don't know what will happen then. Maybe someone will find out what the late Dr Franklin was really getting up to, in that hidden valley, and the true story of our adventure will come out. Maybe not.

Maybe we should tell someone. Dr Franklin's dead, but Skinner's still alive. What if he decides to carry on with the 'great work'? But we don't think he will. We don't think he'll dare. We think he's learned his lesson. And we don't think those technicians and orderlies would be so crazily obedient again. It's simpler if nobody knows.

We don't want to be treated as freaks. Arnie says, 'I'm too young to have my own chat show' – which is typical Arnie, but we're afraid of something worse than becoming tv celebrities. We're afraid if anyone knew *what we are,* they wouldn't be able to bear to leave us alone. They'd want to keep us locked up. They'd want to take samples, do tests, experiment on us. No thanks. We've had enough of that.

So far we've managed to avoid medical check-ups. The nuns in Menozes didn't bother us with doctors, they simply put us to bed and fed us good food. When we got to Quito we said we were fine, and we haven't heard any more about it.

We don't know what will happen when we get home. We look almost normal on the outside. Arnie came out bald, like me, but otherwise unmarked. Miranda has a head of short dark hair, thick and fine as velvet pile, that looks as if it's been oiled. It grows into a point far down on the nape of her neck; and her fingernails are curved like claws. She'll have to avoid stepping on scales in public for a while, because she doesn't weigh much. Arnie, on the other hand, is very heavy for his size. As for me, my gills have sealed over. You can hardly tell they were there. But my eyesight is still perfect (I don't know how I'm going to explain that); and my ears are strange. Arnie and I are going to say we had to have our heads shaved, because our hair was in such a mess. I'll have to wear a hat until my hair grows. Or until my earlobes grow back.

Quito is a wonderful city, by the way. Very high up, and cool, and full of amazing buildings and art. I'd like to come back here some day.

So that's it. The adventure is over. But whatever we look like on the outside, there's something we all three know. *We are not back the way we were before.* Once you've been made transgenic, you stay transgenic. The different DNA is lurking in our cells. Arnie talks about 'flashbacks'. He says the plan was for two kinds of transformation. One where you buy the effect for a few weeks; and the other kind, the proper transgenics who would be reversible, like jumpers. One side human, one side trans – and able to switch between the two. We were meant to be the second type.

213

Now that we've had both halves of the treatment we should be able to switch, though we're not sure how.

I haven't said anything to the others, but I think salt water is my key.

They haven't said anything to me, but I think Arnie knows, and Miranda knows, the triggers that will change them.

We still have the radio telepathy, but we're not using it. We'd rather talk aloud. I think that ability will fade, too. But I think we'll be able to call it back, if we need it.

The phone rings. Miranda picks it up. 'Okay,' I hear her say, 'we're on our way down.'

We don't have much luggage. We pick up the carrier bags that hold the things people bought for the teenage castaways. Toothbrushes, a few spare clothes, underwear. We stand looking at each other, in this last room of the adventure, remembering all the other rooms, and all the horrors; and further back, to the beach, the notch-cutting coconut palm, the waterfall pool . . . the night of the plane wreck. Memories that will last forever.

I thought about shy-nerdy girl, and wondered if my Mum and Dad would miss her.

Maybe she'll grow back, like my hair. Or maybe not.

'What are we?' I asked Miranda. 'Are we monsters? Or are we more than human?'

She shook her head. 'I don't know,' she said. 'You're you. I'm me. Let's go.'

Coda

I know that we can transform again. I believe it will happen, some way, somehow. I think about breathing water, and swimming through the music of the ocean. I think about having a skeleton of supple cartilage instead of brittle bone. I think about feeling my whole body as one soaring, gliding, sweeping wing. I know that Miranda will never forget being able to fly. I dream of another planet, with an ocean of heavy air, where I can swim and she can fly, where we can be the marvellous creatures that we became; and be free, together, with no bars between us. I wonder if it exists, somewhere, out there . . .

Also by Ann Halam

The Powerhouse

'The face looked at Maddy. I saw its empty eyes gleam . . . Somebody screamed and screamed. I think it was me.'

Robs, Jef and Maddy: three friends who just wanted to make music together. How could one summer change their lives the way it did? Maddy and Robs survived, but only just. And the nightmare that happened in the Powerhouse will live with them forever.

'superbly packaged horror' *Books Magazine*

'worth twenty Point Horrors' *School Librarian*

The Fear Man

A dreadful secret hangs over the house in Roman Road. What is it that keeps drawing Andrei to it? And what is the unknown presence that seems to be stalking the family? Constantly on the run from a father he had never known, Andrei is living a nightmare. A compelling story of vampires, magicians and creatures of darkness.

'Brilliantly written . . . a very powerful and affecting book' *BBC Radio 4 Treasure Islands*

The Haunting of Jessica Raven

'Darkness. A cold, foul-smelling darkness. Somewhere a child was screaming.'

Mysterious things start happening to Jessica when, on holiday in France, she meets a group of ragged children. She cannot work out where they come from, but when she meets their leader, an older boy called Jean-Luc, she begins to realise that they may hold the key to her brother's fatal illness.

'. . . a novel of singular completeness and perfection. With it Ann Halam confirms her standing as one of the most exciting of emerging talents' *Junior Bookshelf*

Crying in the Dark

'She didn't know why she had such a strange feeling that they shouldn't have left her alone – but suddenly she understood what the ghosts were trying to tell her. She could make the Madisons wish they'd never been born . . .'

Bullied and abused by her adoptive family Elinor retreats into the restless, vengeful past that haunts their seventeenth-century home. At first it's a way to escape, but soon she's a prisoner and the price of her freedom is something too terrible to contemplate.

'An excellent and compelling ghost story . . .' *The Guardian*

The N.I.M.R.O.D. Conspiracy

'Dear Mum – I'm wedged under the sea-defences, most of me has been eaten by the fishes. Love, Stacey' . . .

Stacey vanished three years ago. She's dead. It's Alan's fault. He knows. But Mum refuses to believe it – her endless search for her little daughter leads them first to NIMROD, and then into a criminal underworld of deceit and conspiracies, burglary, blackmail and terrible danger. NIMROD wields a mysterious power. But *who* are they really? What do they know about Stacey? What can they possibly want from Alan and his Mum?

'a chilling, exciting story' *Our Schools Magazine*

Don't Open Your Eyes

Blood red eyes. Bare bone. Ragged, rotting flesh. No escape.

Something awful has happened to Martin. You'd think it would be all over – after the joyriding, the crash, Martin's tragic death. He was only fifteen.

But Diesel, who was so desperate to make sure that Martin's final resting place was somewhere he feels safe, knows this is just the start of something too terrifying even to think about.

WARNING: DON'T OPEN YOUR EYES unless you are sure you dare read this utterly spine-chilling horror story.